Living Image

Living Image

GLADYS S. GALLANT

DOUBLEDAY & COMPANY, INC.

GARDEN CITY, NEW YORK

1978

All of the characters in this book
are fictitious, and any resemblance
to actual persons, living or dead,
is purely coincidental.

Library of Congress Cataloging in Publication Data

Gallant, Gladys S
Living image.

I. Title.
PZ4.G1624Li [PS3557.A41167] 813'.5'4
ISBN: 0-385-13651-x
Library of Congress Catalog Card Number 77-15178

First Edition

*For my parents, Beth and Martin Selverne,
and for Graig Farrell Weich*

CHAPTER 1

It seemed strange to begin at the end. Karen was dead. Glimmering lights eighteen thousand feet below turned the earth into a neon mosaic. Edith stared out the window of the plane and wondered if she dared tamper with the finality of death. She fingered the newspaper clipping in her hand. It was dated May 11. Exactly four months ago. But she knew the words well. The small print by now had been etched indelibly inside of her. "Wife of famous industrialist, a suicide. Karen Hewlitt, age 32, dies of poison."

Why? A silent question. A haunting question. Fragile, evocative, taunting. "Why" had become the power in the darkness. "Why" had become a relentless virulent disease that permeated the last four months of Edith's existence. It hung like a shadow on every step she took, on every word she wrote. Her career as a fashion editor for *La Mode* . . . the ten carefree years she lived in Paris . . . the framework of that part of her life built on the substance of desire alone, shattered like a nebulous bubble into a million fragments because of her sister's suicide.

She leaned back against the pillow of her seat and smiled gently as she recalled the friends, the lovers, the laughter of Paris that gave emotional context to her new and carefree life. It was ironic that finally the direction she was taking now was controlled by Karen even after death . . . just the way it used to be when they were children together and later. Karen, exquisitely delicate, self-assured with the knowledge that Edith was always there as a bulwark of strength to cushion her life against any form of ugliness. And Edith . . . so helplessly enmeshed in this dependency that her primary function on earth was to achieve fulfillment for Karen. She had served Karen as a human filter through which only the desirable flowed. And for these services rendered, the only return she received was Karen's contempt.

A voice came over the loudspeaker.

"We are now approaching Kennedy Airport in New York and will arrive in approximately ten minutes. We hope that you enjoyed your flight. It has been a pleasure to serve you. Please fasten your seat belts and observe the no smoking sign. Please remain seated until the plane comes to a halt. Thank you."

The lighted mosaic of earth was coming closer. Edith put the newspaper clipping back in her bag and looked at her watch. Ten more minutes. Ten more minutes and the nightmare of Karen's death would become an intense reality that she must face. Ten minutes closer to the truth. It was too late to turn back now. She had tried so hard to shut it out completely and irrevocably. She had reminded herself again and again that she owed nothing to Karen in life, certainly not in death. But the conscionable fact persisted that this was her sister who had died. The mantle of responsibility was not to be cast aside wantonly upon impulse or desire.

Edith pulled a lipstick out of her bag and streaked it across her lips. At last she could manage to smile. The fear she had lived with these last four months was the unknown. That phase of her life was behind her now. The decision to probe it was a relief. She had clung to every moment of these past ten years because she knew it for what it was. An exquisite escape that couldn't last forever. But she wasn't prepared for the way it ended. The ending that Karen, an ocean away, had written with her own hand.

Where will I start? Edith wondered. Where will I find the form and meaning to a senseless tragedy? Why should Karen, the perpetual recipient of pleasure, deal herself the excruciating, painful thrust of death?

When I know these answers I will sleep again. I will dream dreams instead of nightmares. Then I can go back.

But then perhaps there would be no need to go back, to escape anymore. The probing of Karen's death might ultimately give form to her own life that had no form. Could it be that Karen's ending would trigger her own beginning?

She stared out the window again. The plane turned and a gleaming spotlight blazed on the wing, almost blinding her. The long line of approach lights was clearly visible now in the darkness. The plane settled for the landing, then rolled along the runway between the flares of light.

She was home after ten years, if this could be called home. The runway lights swept by and the plane eased gently to the ground to meet them.

Edith walked out of the plane onto the passenger ramp leading to the customs area. She scanned the baggage belt for her suitcases, desolately conscious of the crowds of people waving from above. There was no family, no friend, no familiar face straining anxiously through the night searching for her face. She was alone in her pursuit of a nightmare. She shuddered involuntarily although the September evening was warm, merely punctuated by slight breezes from outside brushing against her hair and rustling her dark dress.

She went through customs rapidly. She had traveled light from Paris because she had only intended to remain in New York for two months.

A man standing next to her caught her eyes and smiled . . . someone who had been on the plane. But she moved away. She was used to men staring at her, turning to look at her as she walked down a street, although she could never understand why.

The very things she hated about herself heightened her appeal . . . a definite lack of certainty in her manner, an apologetic air, an unsureness that she felt always betrayed itself and made her unattractive. She wasn't aware that there was something else about her . . . an invisible yet apparent sensuality that came through in the fluent way she walked, in the way she held her head, the way she smiled. It was even in her voice. The very fusion of the sophisticated and naïve, softness and burning fire, unawareness and awareness . . . these were the elements that made many men turn and stare, and made many women wonder what men saw in her.

She remembered how most people used to liken her vaguely to Karen, but she was sure she paled by the comparison. Karen was a startling, striking beauty with her deep green eyes and soft red hair. She was vivid, exciting. Edith's quiet brunette coloring merely served to set Karen's appearance into sharper focus when they were together. Edith was the backdrop, the foil, the audience who enhanced Karen's dynamics. But that was a long time ago, a lifetime ago. Now she was back again but Karen would never be back. Edith knew she must re-create a lapse of ten years in two months, and she wondered how it could be possible.

A porter took her luggage to a line of waiting taxis. She had no plans other than to go to a hotel and then begin. Try to begin. She didn't have a starting point. But somewhere in the maze of New York there were people who had known Karen, had loved Karen, had lived with Karen. Karen would have left a mark on some of them, maybe all of them—a mark that could not be erased. She must find those particular ones whom Karen had reached, the ones with whom Karen had been involved. Some of them must know the answers. Some would know what had happened to Karen and why.

CHAPTER 2

It was a room that dealt with life and death, murder and suicide. Edith Weston sat on a worn leather chair, forming her own appraisal of the man opposite her. He was a large hulking man somewhere in his fifties, with sparse light hair and a ruddy face. The brass bars on his uniform designated his rank, but the steady penetrating eyes designated the man. He gave the morbid anatomy of the room a sense of solidity that was extremely comforting. The man was Lieutenant Gerard. The office was the Homicide Division of the New York Police Department.

"So after ten years you've returned to New York, Miss Weston." Gerard tapped the folder on his desk. "I regret the circumstances that brought you back."

"I came as soon as I could," Edith said. "As soon as I could take a leave of absence."

Gerard leaned forward and opened the manila file on his desk. "As a matter of fact," he said quietly, "we expected you much sooner."

"You did?"

Gerard nodded. "We knew Karen Hewlitt had a sister in Paris. But the records show that Mrs. Hewlitt's maiden name was De Witt," he said.

"Yes. She changed it legally while she was working as a model," Edith said.

"It took some time to discover you, Miss Weston," Gerard said. "Mrs. Hewlitt's past was . . . well, you might say submerged. By the time we located you at *La Mode* magazine you were already on your way to America. We had been told there were no relatives."

"Except for myself," Edith said. "We were orphans."

"Of course it would be extremely difficult to deny the relationship if you had lived here. There's quite a resemblance."

Edith flushed. "I don't think Karen was trying to deny anything. It's just that . . . well . . ."

"Just what?"

"I've been away for ten years. We used to write every once in a while, but after I left for Paris we were never as close, that's all," she said.

"Then why did you come back?" Gerard asked softly.

"I read about the . . . the suicide in an American newspaper. It seemed . . . strange. Out of context with someone like Karen. If you knew her . . . anyone who knew her would realize it just doesn't make sense. She had everything. She always had everything." Edith took a deep breath and went on softly. "And she was everything. Beautiful, clever, magnetic. Why would she kill herself?"

A faint smile hovered on Gerard's mouth. "I assume," he said, "that's a rhetorical question. You don't expect me to answer it, do you?"

"It doesn't make sense," Edith said again.

"It has to make sense, Miss Weston, because the fact remains . . . she's dead. She poisoned herself." Gerard tapped the folder on his desk. "It's all here, all on paper . . . the coroner's report . . . the testimony at the inquest. The proof is here." He rested his hand on the folder and glanced at her. "You may see it if you wish," he added kindly, "but spare yourself the details. Take my word for it."

Edith nodded silently and opened her pocketbook. "Here's one fact you don't have, Lieutenant Gerard." She pulled an envelope from her bag and held it toward him. "The last letter she wrote to me." Edith placed the letter on Gerard's desk. "Perhaps the proof is on this paper—not that one," she said in a strained voice.

Gerard picked up the envelope. The expression on his face was bland as he carefully withdrew the sheet of paper covered with delicate slanted writing. Karen Hewlitt had written the date, May 9, at the top of the page. Gerard glanced back to the postmark stamped on the envelope. Edith Weston had received this letter on May 12, two days after Karen Hewlitt had died. Gerard's eyes moved back again to the expensive stiffish white paper in his hand: "Edith . . . I'm sorry I haven't written sooner. Things have a way of getting so complicated and complications take up time. The honeymoon is over. But then how could it be over when it never really began? You don't have to read between the lines to know what I mean. I'm through with Mike. He gave me a rough time about the divorce,

but I can't take no for an answer. I guess I never could . . .
remember? Of course there's another man. Exciting, wonderful, everything I've ever wanted. This honeymoon is going to take us to
Paris. Look for us there at Christmastime. I'm looking forward to
seeing you again at last. Ten years is a long time. Karen."

Nothing changed in Gerard's expression. He folded the paper
neatly, returned it to the envelope, then held it close up against his
face. Edith stared at him and Gerard half closed his eyes. The only
sound in the room was the intermittent ring of a telephone somewhere outside the office.

"You can still smell the faint aroma of perfume," he said softly.
"Even after all these months. I recall that fragrance. It was there in
the bedroom when we found her. That perfume clings to my mind
just the way it clings to this letter." Gerard reached automatically
for a cigar. "You don't mind the smoke?" he asked.

"I don't mind." Edith was still staring at him.

Gerard leaned back in his swivel chair and returned her glance. It
was intercepted only by the thick stream of smoke that spilled out
from the brown cigar Gerard held in his strong fingers.

A sudden perception hit her. "You . . . you don't believe it was
suicide either," she said all at once. "You haven't believed it from
the first. Even before I showed you this letter." The tone of his
voice, the expression on his face gave her the clue. She knew she
was right.

"Now whatever gave you that idea?" he said, his sharp eyes still
concentrating upon her without deviation.

"She was murdered. Karen was murdered. You know it, don't
you?" The words were half whispered, almost imploring in their
demand for the truth.

Gerard placed the letter in the folder. "You're wrong there, Miss
Weston. I don't know it. I only know the facts, the proven facts."

"But that letter . . . doesn't that prove . . . ?"

"That letter proves nothing. She planned to remarry, go to Paris
on a honeymoon, but then something happened. She changed her
mind."

"So she decided to kill herself instead," Edith said in a voice
traced with sarcasm. "Really, Lieutenant."

Gerard stood up abruptly. In this sudden movement his huge
frame had taken over the office completely. "The case is closed,

Miss Weston. The police are satisfied with the investigation and my superiors are satisfied."

"And you?"

Gerard sighed and moved from behind the desk. He placed his hand across his stomach. The gesture was almost a ludicrous one except for the pained expression in his eyes. "I get it here," he said. "Right here. In the stomach. A strange sensation that has nothing to do with digestion. I get it every time I feel something's wrong with a case. It hits me right here. Only at night. Keeps me up. Stay here a week and see the sights, Miss Weston. Live. Have yourself a time. Then go back to Paris. Forget it."

"Won't you tell me the names of her friends? At least tell me how I can reach her husband," Edith persisted. "It's impossible to see him. I've been trying all week."

Gerard frowned. "You're going to give me trouble, aren't you? I knew it the minute you walked into this room."

Edith regarded him indignantly. "I've come all the way from Paris to find out what happened to my sister and you tell me to stay a week and go sight-seeing!"

"Miss Weston," Gerard said with a last vestige of patience, "why don't you face the facts? A Homicide investigation has no time for stray hunches."

"I just want to meet the people she knew," Edith insisted stubbornly.

Gerard's voice suddenly boomed out angrily as he threw the words back at her. "You just want to meet the people she knew! You just want some simple introductions. All very casual. Just nosying around in a social sort of way. Okay." He slammed his fist down on the desk. "Maybe you think you'll have a ball moving around in your sister's social set. You figure you've come all the way from Paris, so you want some action. Miss Weston . . . if that hunch just happens to be right . . . you're going to get it. You're going to meet your sister's murderer face to face!"

"What . . . what do you mean?" The words came out hoarsely, incredulously.

"I mean your life may be in danger. You may end up dead in some lonely hotel room. An apparent suicide. Or maybe your lifeless form will be sprawled in the street. A victim of an unknown hit-and-run driver. It could happen in a thousand places in a thousand ways. It could happen anytime." He lowered his voice and the whispered words clung to the silent room. "If it happened to her . . . it could happen to you."

Edith stared at him in horror. "Her murderer kill me? But . . . why?"

"Because he's a clever one. Clever enough to avoid detection, even suspicion. He'll know what you're up to. He'll stalk your footsteps. He'll watch your every move. He'll be waiting for you somewhere . . . a dark street corner, an empty apartment. He'll be waiting. If he killed once he could kill again. We could be dealing with a paranoid. We don't even know if it's a man or a woman. And you want an introduction."

"But the police . . . couldn't the police give me some sort of protection?"

"For what reason? A hunch? The Hewlitt case is closed," Gerard said. "You and I are the only ones who suspect it may be something other than suicide. If we're right, then only one of us may be alive to prove it. The police won't come in on this case . . . until you're dead." Gerard's face was damp with anger. He leaned over and picked up a pencil and scrawled something on a piece of paper. "Here." He handed the paper to her. "I can't stop you from seeing her husband. And here's the address of Alan Prescott, a friend. You'd find out for yourself if I didn't tell you. Meet them if you must. But don't mention the letter you gave me to anyone."

Edith's face was white as she took the slip of paper and placed it in her bag.

"Go away, Miss Weston," Gerard said, wearily moving back to the desk. "Go away. Do what you want. My insomnia is bad enough without you. Go away. But remember . . . I warned you. What you're asking for . . . is an introduction to death."

CHAPTER 3

Alan Prescott stared apprehensively at the three large windows in his office. This usually gave him a feeling of comfort and security. The three windows had a commanding view of the Triborough Bridge and the East River. It took a lot of doing to rate a three-window office at Chanin and Chanin Advertising, 30 Rockefeller Plaza. It took a lot out of his expense account. And it took a lot out of his guts. Lately, when he noticed his thinning hair that was camouflaged in a boyish hair cut and his lean face now slightly furrowed with faint lines, he saw nothing more than a well-tailored procurer. But this recent discomforting appraisal was quickly replaced by: Hell, you've got to sacrifice something.

Ordinarily, he found the advertising business stimulating. It was a colossal chess game played for super-colossal stakes, and he'd done all right. An eighty-thousand-dollar-a-year man and he was forty-seven years old. But there was no margin for error in this business. And he had made one mistake. Karen Hewlitt. His only mistake since reaching the three-window plateau.

Alan frowned and walked over to his desk. He pressed the buzzer and almost instantly his secretary appeared.

"Yes, Mr. Prescott?"

Pat smiled ingratiatingly at him. She was a dark brunette from Memphis, Tennessee, who invariably wore demure high-necked dresses pulled taut across her breasts and hips. She'd been there nearly two months and he knew from the start that just a minimum of response in her direction would wind up in a short dinner and a long night.

But with Karen . . . it was different with a woman like Karen. She was different. Beautiful. Yes, she was beautiful, but so are a lot of women. It was something else that came through. A certain intensity, an urgency about her that charged the atmosphere with electricity. When she entered a room every audience became a captive one. You had to notice her and admire her and . . . want her.

"Yes, Mr. Prescott?" Pat was being tenuously patient.

Alan pulled himself back to the present. "Are you sure there was no memo from J.C.?"

"No, sir. It would have been on your desk."

"I know a board meeting about the Hewlitt account was scheduled for late today. Maybe a call came through while you were taking your coffee break."

"I didn't take a coffee break, Mr. Prescott," Pat said in an injured tone. "Would you like me to check with Mr. Chanin's secretary?"

"No, don't bother."

Alan already knew that the revolving door had started to revolve and he was right there in it. He could see the exit sign already. The Hewlitt Auto account was the biggest one on the books. He ought to know. He was the account executive. But now the Hewlitt motorcars were shifting into high gear off in another direction. As of one night four months ago. As of the night Karen Hewlitt was found dead. A suicide. It was still too incredibly shocking for complete absorption.

Even now he could see her face, hear her low soft voice. It made an invitation out of everything she said. And she said she was lonely. Her husband was always working. Hell, he knew what she was up to—he ought to. It was his game she was playing. But the way she played it—it was fascinating.

At first, he laughed at her. Then he stopped laughing because he began to fall in love with her. That was what she wanted. Karen always got what she wanted. She became even more beautiful, more irresistible, more magnetic . . . until he threw away what was left of his book of rules.

When he held her in his arms she felt warm and soft and there was something so helpless and fragile about her he was afraid she would shatter into a million fragments. When you got real close she was mercury. Did you ever put your finger on mercury? Shining elusive silver that clung for only moments, then vanished.

But those moments were magic. Then there was no night, no world. Just a deep and moving vacuum holding the two of them in a special kind of oneness.

"Mr. Prescott?" Pat came back into the room. "I spoke to Mr. Chanin's secretary anyway. There was a board meeting this afternoon. But . . ." She let it hang in the air regretfully. It didn't take long at Chanin and Chanin Advertising to know what the score was. Even a secretary.

"Oh." Alan reached for a cigarette. So this was it. "There's no sense waiting around, Pat. It's after six already."

"Are you sure there isn't anything else?" She stood there uncertainly.

"No, you go home. In fact, there's no sense in my waiting around now either."

"Well . . . good night then, Mr. Prescott. See you in the morning."

"Good night, Pat."

He started to close up his desk as Tom Belding charged through the door.

"Geez, what a meeting. The old man was ripping."

Tom flung himself into the leather chair and let out a long slow whistle. He was one of the contact men who moved over from CBS a year ago. A species who periodically managed to get shifted from agency to network every time a big new account was lost, sold, or stolen. He could chalk up five different positions in six years. But his ruddy, beaming face and outgoing exuberance belied his forty-odd years and intrinsic insecurity.

"What happened to you, boy?" he bellowed. "Thought the Hewlitt account was your baby."

Alan tightened. The first thing he needed was a drink. The last thing he needed was Tom Belding. So he said, "How about a drink, Tom?"

Maybe the combination of both would dilute his awareness into an innocuous state of limbo. "What do you say, boy?" He approximated Tom's gusto.

They walked over to La Grange and nodded to several of the Madison Avenue commuters at the bar. After two quick ones Alan managed to say casually, "So the meeting was a steam bath."

"Understatement of the year." Tom grinned. "Chanin's getting desperate. Hewlitt's slipping right through his fingers."

"Too bad I missed the show," Alan said dryly.

"It figures, boy, doesn't it?" Tom nudged him to underscore the question.

"I don't follow you."

"Four months ago, wasn't it, when they found her?"

"What are you talking about?"

"What everybody's talking about." He let the name drop casually. "Karen Hewlitt."

"That's past history, Tom." Alan's hand was shaking. He gripped the glass tighter. Was that the sound of his own voice? Guilty? Choked? Tense? He signaled for another drink. In another minute Belding would be spelling it out.

"I don't have to tell you, Alan. You're the one who can fill me in. You were the"—he took a slow beat, then: "the friend of the family." Tom smiled ingratiatingly.

"I don't like your insinuations, Belding." Alan's words spilled out thickly.

"Man, you've had too much to drink." Belding wasn't grinning now.

Alan pulled a ten-dollar bill out of his pocket and threw it on the counter. Tom sat there staring at him as Alan picked up his hat, walked rapidly toward the door and out into the street.

It started to rain as he crossed Madison Avenue at Fifty-second Street and headed east toward Park Avenue. He checked his watch with the clock on the Grand Central Building. Seven o'clock and the traffic jam was still going strong. He passed Morgen's and Café Richelieu and the crush of people standing at the corners trying to flag taxis. But he wasn't thinking about the dinnertime rush hour or the bright lights. He saw it all through the wrong end of a telescope . . . it looked small, far away. The wrong perspective. That was it. He had the wrong perspective. He was starting to slip. Maybe he was cracking up, going to pieces. He was starting to slip, all right. One mistake after another. He had always prided himself on his calculations.

The cool evening air and the falling rain started to clear his head. He shouldn't have said that to Tom. Of course, Belding didn't make much difference one way or another. Still—what he said about Karen. That made a lot of difference. Belding knew what was going on. That's how Belding kept his head above water. By knowing what was going on. He wasn't smart. But he always kept his fingers on the pulse. Belding said the others were talking. It was dangerous talk. Alan had a curious sensation that everything was closing in on him. The beginning of the end. But where did the end begin? Why should he feel so uneasy? So Karen Hewlitt committed suicide. Why should he feel guilty? Hell, it wasn't his fault.

Alan walked over to Second Avenue, then started downtown. Why should I feel responsible? He started to walk faster now as the rain came pouring down. So he had had an affair with another man's wife. Big deal. It happens every minute of every hour of every day. So what? But why, why did it have to be Mike Hewlitt's wife?

A cab pulled up and a young couple got out in front of a restaurant called Sempiones. Damn. He was supposed to be at the Martins' cocktail party tonight.

"Taxi!" he called out just as the cab started to move away. The cab backed up and slowed to a stop. Alan opened the door and hopped in. He gave the driver the address. It was No. 2 Sutton Place South. He wondered if Mike Hewlitt would be there. Maybe over a few drinks he and Mike . . . no, it wouldn't work. Mike wasn't seeing many people these days. Especially Alan Prescott, persona non grata. Mike wouldn't be there anyway. Maybe the Swansons would be there. An important link with the Manhattan Textile Mills. What was Swanson's wife's name? Beulah? Betty? Barbara? He was sure it began with a "B" anyway. Barbara. That was it. He pulled out a cigarette and lit it. To hell with it! He wasn't going to get caught up in that rat race again. He'd had it. Right up to the neck. He inhaled deply and leaned back against the cushion of the seat as the taxi made a left turn and rapidly joined the mass of cars surging uptown on First Avenue.

CHAPTER 4

Alan fumbled for his door key. Two A.M. and too many bourbons. He never should have gone to the Martins' cocktail party in the first place. It was too much of everything. Too late. Too many people. Too much noise. The Swansons were there, all right, but her name wasn't Barbara after all. It was Betty. And there was too much of Betty Swanson too.

It wasn't until he was halfway into his living room that he noticed a woman in the dim light, among the shadows. She was seated on the sofa smoking a cigarette. Alan stopped and stared. That was all he could do. He couldn't move. All he could think of was—Karen. This woman was Karen. Don't panic, he warned himself. It was that last drink. A trick of the imagination. A cruel trick of the shadows in the night.

"I'm sorry," she said. "I didn't mean to frighten you." Her voice was low, husky.

He switched on the lamp next to the bar. Even in the clearer light there was a striking resemblance to Karen. The delicate features, the tilt of the nose, the high cheekbones. But the eyes were different. Soft, luminous, deep brown with thick curling lashes. And the hair —that was different too. A dark cloud framing a porcelain white face. Alan looked into her eyes and smiled with relief.

"I'm sorry," she said again. She sounded like music in a minor key.

"For a moment there, I could have sworn you were somebody else." Christ, he was shaking. He sat down on the chair opposite her and tried to steady his voice. "Why don't you join me in a drink while you tell me what you're doing here?"

"That's a wonderful idea."

He went to the liquor cabinet and set up two glasses. "Scotch? Bourbon? What'll you have?"

"Whatever you're having."

He poured two short drinks and handed her one. He downed his quickly. "That's better. In those shadows I thought I was seeing things. You are for real, aren't you? You didn't just suddenly materialize?"

"Your maid let me in just before she left. I told her I was a friend."

"And you've been waiting here all these hours?" he asked incredulously.

"I've been waiting for weeks," she answered, "so you see, a few more hours don't really make any difference."

"Even if you're a housebreaker I forgive you completely," Alan said. "It isn't often that I find a beautiful woman waiting for me to come home."

As he spoke he was making some rapid mental calculations. He figured her physical similarity to Karen Hewlitt was too close to be coincidental. Obviously she had poise and intelligence, but despite her apparent composure there was an underlying quality of apprehension—or was it urgency?—that made her unannounced visit even more mystifying. He decided to get to the heart of the matter quickly. He walked to the desk and deliberately picked up the framed photograph of Karen.

"Did you know you almost had a double?" He watched her carefully as he spoke.

She answered quietly. "Just in the photograph. I saw the picture while I waited for you. We never really looked that much alike."

"Who are you?" For a long moment the question hung in the air. The stillness in the room was suffocating.

Then she answered evenly, "Karen was my sister. My name is Edith Weston."

"Your sister . . . ?"

"Didn't you know?"

"The longer I knew Karen, the less I knew about her."

"But I thought that you—"

Alan interrupted. "Let me put it this way. I was . . . just a friend of the family."

She stood up and moved slowly toward the window. Out there, Edith thought, out there was the city in all its impenetrable blackness. It would never yield any of the answers she wanted. It must be here. She turned and looked at him. "What happened, Mr. Prescott? What happened to Karen?"

"I wish to God I knew," he said.

Another dead-end street, she thought. Another maze that ends up nowhere.

"If you're her sister," he went on, "surely you—"

"I haven't seen Karen in the last ten years," she said. "Ten years is a long time. I've been working in Paris as a fashion editor for *La Mode*. We used to write once in a while. But even with letters you lose touch." She sounded almost frightened. "After all, there was a whole ocean between us."

Alan detected the note of fear in her voice. He wondered about it. Why was she so afraid? Afraid of what? Of whom? But these past four months he was on edge, nervous, jumpy. He knew he was overreacting to everything. Even the remark that Tom Belding made in the bar. But why did she come to him?

"What about your family?" he asked her suspiciously.

"There is no family. Karen and I were orphans," she said. "I know you're wondering why I came here, how I had the nerve to barge in this way." She stopped, visibly embarrassed. "I had to, Mr. Prescott. There was no one else."

Alan's face relaxed. She looked helpless. Obviously housebreaking wasn't her vocation. "Did you try the police?" he asked her.

"The police?" She hesitated imperceptibly. "No," she lied deliberately. "There didn't seem to be any point in that. This is more of a personal matter."

"Then how did you get my name?"

"Karen wrote me about you some time ago," she improvised hastily. "She just mentioned that you were a friend of her husband's. Oh, I tried to contact Mike Hewlitt. I've been calling him all week. But I found there can also be personal Iron Curtains. And Mike Hewlitt is behind one of them." She shook her head hopelessly.

Yes, Alan thought, Mike Hewlitt had dropped the Iron Curtain after the night Karen died. He hadn't seen or spoken to Mike in months. All he heard around the agency was that Hewlitt was going to resign the account. He'd like to break through that Iron Curtain himself, before he lost his job. Maybe there was a way to break through. Maybe this girl . . . maybe she could provide the wedge. Or better still, maybe she herself could be the wedge. Maybe with her he could start the wheels spinning all over again. Those three windows in his office loomed larger and larger. His whole career was at stake.

Hewlitt had gone to strange extremes to weave his shroud of silence after Karen's death. Why? What really happened the night Karen died? What did Edith Weston know? Maybe Hewlitt blamed him for what happened. But how could he? Karen's audience of admirers added up to S.R.O.—Standing Room Only. Or maybe Hewlitt blamed himself for what happened. His jealousy . . . his refusal to give her a divorce . . . she couldn't take it anymore, so she took poison instead. Or . . . was poisoned? No. Hewlitt couldn't have gone that far. If he did, then let him keep his shroud of silence. Otherwise, there wouldn't be any account to reinstate.

It wouldn't do to blow up a storm. But what if there were reverberations about the suicide? Just subtle hints to Mike Hewlitt . . . infinitesimal specks of doubt and suspicion . . . to what extent would Hewlitt go to keep that shroud intact? Why, Hewlitt wouldn't have to go to any extreme at all. He'd just have to pick up the phone and reinstate the account. Not blackmail, just bargaining power. All part of the game. But Alan would have to play it smart. Courtesy of Edith Weston, perhaps?

He offered her a cigarette and said, "How long have you been in this country, Miss Weston?"

"Just about two weeks."

"But you said you were out of touch with your sister"—he leaned closer toward her—"so how did you know she died?"

Edith reached for her handbag and pulled the worn clipping out. "News travels," she said, "particularly about the wife of a famous industrialist."

Alan looked at the clipping, deflated. It was from an American paper, dated May 11, the day after she died. Edith Weston knew nothing. He stamped his cigarette out in the ashtray. "My advice to you, Miss Weston, is to go back." His idea was nothing more than a pipe dream. "You say there was a whole ocean between you? There was a whole world between you! Go back," he said abruptly. "You're wasting your time."

For a moment tears flooded her eyes, then she quickly regained her composure. "Perhaps you're right, Mr. Prescott. But I'm not going back. I must find out what happened."

The urgency in her voice, her manner. There it was again. She must know something. She must suspect something more than suicide.

"Is there something else you're trying to tell me?"

She took a cigarette from her pocketbook and he struck a match, holding the flame to the tip. He noticed that her hand was trembling. "No," she replied. "Nothing else. Except that it all seemed so curious, so shocking . . . for someone like Karen. She was always so certain about what she wanted, so sure of herself." She paused and drew on the cigarette. "How could she kill herself, Mr. Prescott?"

Alan shook his head. "Perhaps on a sudden destructive impulse . . ." he murmured.

"I never remembered her as being impulsive."

"No," he agreed. "You could hardly call Karen that."

"Then why? I must find out what happened!"

"To do that," Alan said, "you would have to reconstruct her whole life with Mike Hewlitt. And that's trying to work a jigsaw puzzle without the parts."

"But you knew them both. You could tell me. You must tell me about Karen," she said.

Karen. How could anybody describe her? Karen was the bright lights on a marquee. Shining and glowing. Karen was the music of a torch song. Sad and lovely and lonely.

"You must tell me," Edith said again.

He could only reply, "You're her sister. You tell me."

"I only wish I could," she said. "Ten years can be a lifetime. Like you said, there was a whole world between us."

He lit another cigarette and remembered. "When Karen walked into a room, she owned it," he said. "She was the kind of woman any man would want . . . and no man would forget. That's what Karen was like."

"You . . . you loved her?" she said softly.

He looked up sharply. "What made you say that?"

"The tone of your voice . . . the way you looked."

"I told you. I was nothing more than a friend of the family."

"But what about Mike Hewlitt? Couldn't you arrange to have me meet him?"

"You never saw him?"

"I'm sure he doesn't even know I exist."

"But surely Karen told him about you," Alan said.

"I'm sure she didn't." It was so typical of Karen to obliterate Edith's existence. She was never important enough for Karen's world. But Edith only said, "We were apart for so many years."

Alan thought for a moment before he spoke. There was a chance, just a slim one, but a chance that maybe Edith Weston could get through to Mike Hewlitt. If she could get close enough to Mike . . . Alan looked at her abruptly. It was a long shot. Still he'd have to take it. A well-calculated risk. "Maybe," he said, "maybe I could arrange a meeting between you and Mike. Maybe he would talk to you."

"Could you?" For the first time she smiled at him. It was like someone turning on an electric light. "I would be so grateful if you did. It means so much to me."

"I'll see what I can do."

"Thank you." She rose and started toward the door. "I won't keep you any longer. I hope you'll forgive the intrusion."

Alan watched her as she moved. She even had the same body as Karen, lithe, firm, seductive. Edith Weston, like her sister, was also the kind of woman any man would want.

"Wait," he said, and followed her to the door. "Don't go. Not yet." Her hand was on the doorknob and he covered it with his own.

She drew away.

"I'll arrange that meeting, I promise you. You'll be around for a while?"

"That all depends." She paused, then looked up at him shyly. "On you, I mean."

"Then you can count on it. Where are you staying?"

"The Gotham."

"Let me take you over there. It's very late."

"No, thanks."

"I'll put you in a cab then."

"Thank you, but . . . I'd like to walk a bit. It's just a few blocks and it's stopped raining." She held out her hand. "Goodbye, Mr. Prescott."

"Alan."

"Alan," she repeated.

He took her hand and held it briefly. "But not goodbye. Not by a long shot."

He kept thinking about her after she left. She was beautiful, all right, and appealing. She and Karen—they were almost dead ringers physically, except for the coloring. But emotionally they were different. Edith Weston was warmer, more pliable, with a certain reserve which he suspected stemmed from shyness. He would enjoy a woman like that. It would be interesting. Offbeat for him. The ethereal type. She could get Hewlitt to talk, all right. Maybe he could parlay a beautiful woman and his job into a double winner.

CHAPTER 5

Edith walked over to Fifth Avenue. She had forgotten nighttime in New York, the faint lights, silence, and shadows. It was lonely and frightening. She remembered Gerard's warning and she shivered and walked a little faster. She glanced back over her shoulder. No one was following her. No one was watching her. But then no one knew she was here except Alan Prescott. And her introduction to him could hardly be called an introduction to death. It was a ridiculous notion. Why should anyone want to kill her? The idea was even laughable. Alan Prescott was not only cordial, he was helpful. She almost told him about Gerard, and Karen's letter. Except that she couldn't completely disregard Gerard's warning. He had missed his vocation. He should have been a mystery writer. She smiled and slackened her pace.

All the familiar landmarks she remembered were gone. The newness of the Fifth Avenue buildings surrounding her made her feel strange, an intruder. She had a sudden impulse to turn east and walk over to Lexington and Fiftieth Street, where she and Karen once shared a tiny walk-up. But she was sure that had been replaced too. Probably there was nothing left, but then there had been nothing to leave.

And now there were only the memories. Their ridiculous little apartment . . . the walls papered with match covers from The Stork, Champignon, Orsini's, The 21 Club, Danny's Hideaway, the Press Box, the Rainbow Room, Toots Shore's, the Copa, El Morocco . . . dozens more. Karen really got around. New clubs and the old ones. New men and the old ones. With Karen it was just an endless succession of fast turnovers. The names were a blur even then. Except Paul Levitt. His name was never a blur. Just a poignant reminder of something that could have been and never was . . . Paul Levitt.

"Paul Levitt?" Karen uttered the name with dismay. "*Me*—Mrs. Paul Levitt? Really, Edith." Then she laughed. "Can you see me married to a struggling young lawyer in . . . *Utica?*" Edith couldn't help smiling. The idea was preposterous. "Besides," Karen said, "I wouldn't dream of leaving you all alone in New York." Karen's rationalizations were always superb.

Soon after that Edith was the only one who was ever home to Paul. Then she began to get used to the horn-rimmed glasses and the scent of tweed and tobacco and even the musty old law books he always carted around.

She hadn't meant to fall in love with him. It was sudden and jolting and frightening. It was wrong, all wrong. What right did she have to marry Paul and leave Karen, when Karen rejected him ostensibly for the same reason? It was a curious reversal of circumstances. But there was still another reason. One that she knew but wouldn't admit. She felt guilty about loving Paul. Even though Karen was through with him, he was in love with Karen first.

So she told Paul she wouldn't leave New York, and she couldn't leave Karen alone. They quarreled about it each time they met and then one day they stopped meeting. It ended as fast as it started. The void he left increased as the weeks went by, and it was only filled with the painful realization of how much he meant to her. But it was too late. He already had gone back home to Utica.

Edith knew then she could have no life of her own as long as Karen was in the picture. Her own desires would always be submerged as long as Karen remained the focal point of action. Edith would have to make the break. Someone at her office said *La Mode*, the French fashion magazine, was looking for an American copywriter. It meant going to Paris and living there. She knew Karen wouldn't like the idea at all.

"You must be out of your mind!"

"I've got to make a go of it alone," Edith said. "You don't really need me, Karen. You can get any modeling job . . . anytime. All you have to do is pick up the phone. You can get anything you want."

But Karen did need her. At least until she could find a replacement. So Karen softened her voice to placating innocence. "We've always been together, always shared everything," she said. "I wasn't aware that you were unhappy, Edith."

"You were never aware of anything except yourself," Edith replied evenly. "This job in Paris . . . I'm taking it."

Karen's green eyes glittered with anger. There was only one way she knew—her way. "What's wrong with you anyway? You can't leave. You can't just walk out on me!"

"If I don't break away now I never will."

"Break away from what?" snapped Karen.

"From being your captive audience maybe," Edith said bitterly. "I never had a chance to get anything I wanted." Then she told her about Paul.

"Paul?" Karen looked shocked. "Paul Levitt? That . . . that peasant? He wasn't good enough for me . . . so how could he be good enough for you?"

"I should have married him," Edith said. "But I didn't want to hurt you. And now it's too late. It will happen this way again and again. The only way is to make a break."

"Go ahead and do what you want." Karen's anger finally simmered down to indifference. "But I assure you, you won't find anything different in Paris. Paris can't change you. You'll always be the same old Edith."

Karen's words hurt. And in the beginning Karen was right. It was lonely in Paris and strange, and there was an emptiness without Paul. And then after a long while she began to make a life in Paris. There was a time to live and a time to forget. Edith tried to do both in Paris. Two years later Karen wrote about her marriage to a New York automobile tycoon. There were letters after that about her glittering, fabulous world. Even in her letters Karen had a way of making Edith's life dull by contrast. Then four months ago she opened Karen's last letter.

It was written the day before she died. But why suicide? If Karen was planning to remarry, if she was going to meet Edith again in Paris . . . but a thousand ifs couldn't change the fact, the terrible tragic fact that Karen was dead. Why did she die? Was Alan Prescott in love with her? What was her marriage like? Who was the other man in her life? Was it Alan? Someone else? Who was Mike Hewlitt? A name? A face? A murderer?

She walked slowly up the steps of the Gotham Hotel, asked for her room key at the desk, then rang the bell for the elevator. She would phone Mike Hewlitt again tomorrow.

CHAPTER 6

"Excuse me, sir."

Mike Hewlitt looked up with a start as the butler unobtrusively entered the library.

"What is it, Philip?"

"Mr. Hewlitt, that lady phoned again. She said it was very urgent, sir."

"I told you I'm not taking any phone calls."

"But she said—"

"I don't care what she said. Why do you think this phone is unlisted? How did she get this number?"

"I don't know, sir. It's about the sixth time she called."

"Next time tell her I'm out of town," Mike said shortly.

"Yes, Mr. Hewlitt." The butler left the room as silently as he had entered it.

One of the by-products of money was silence. Mike Hewlitt had known that for a long time. The mansion he lived in now was a shroud of silence. Thick carpets. Silent servants. The hushed atmosphere produced by paneled walls, solid ceilings, gleaming silver, muted tones of antique woods, heavy bronze, unlisted phone numbers, silently chauffeured limousines. He had known silence for a long time, as long as he could remember: even with his parents, whom he only remembered as remote and handsome images of a fabled society, on the estate on Long Island when he was a child, and in the town house in Manhattan very much like the one he was living in now. Time and necessity blurred a further clarification.

He inherited one of the thrones of industry. There was nothing more he could ever attain except more power. Push buttons replaced personal contacts. His money and position precluded honest reactions and relationships. People thought of him as an industry instead of as a human being. As a defense against this he used his money and position to preclude human relationships. He was forced to be on guard against people, publicity, notoriety. The prestige of the Hewlitt name must be maintained at all costs. His position was rigid and he had to pay the price of loneliness. It was an enormous, gigantic price. But he paid it with every breath he took.

Loneliness became his invisible and indestructible companion, smiling at him, taunting him. Loneliness became the temptress who got into his blood, the predatory wife who shared his kingdom of wealth, who waited for him at night when he came home from the office, and who slept in his bed, but would give him nothing in return. She owned more of him than he did. But when he tried to stifle her, choke her out of existence, she became as vital and alive as the soft warm luxurious sables his mother used to wear. He could never quite reach out far enough to hold them. Once, just once in his life he thought he could conquer this woman called loneliness. It was when he met Karen.

Mike got up from his easy chair and walked over to the fireplace and pressed a button. The whole panel above became diffused with light. An oil painting of an exquisite woman suddenly came alive. Mike stepped back from the portrait and the glow of the light shone on the soft white skin. It was a portrait of Karen. One could almost see her breathe. Soft red hair framed the delicate face. The eyes were green flecked with gold. The artist caught their deep impenetrability. She was wearing a yellow satin gown that fell in soft folds from the waist and caught in a swirling drape low at the full, rounded bosom. Karen, the beautiful. Karen, the elusive. Karen, the enigma. All the enticement and the seductiveness were there, captured in every stroke of the painting. Mike caught his breath. Even in this painting she made his heart beat faster, his emotions quicken. He stepped closer to the painting and with his hand he traced the fine texture of her skin, the delicate outline of her face. Karen was the weapon that could conquer loneliness.

He remembered the first night he saw her. It was at a theater benefit. She was sitting next to him and he kept staring at her. She was with some friends of his . . . the Martins. They were introduced. When she spoke to him, her voice was low and throaty, just the way he imagined it.

He saw her every night after that for two weeks. It was a new world, fresh and shining.

At first the relationship had a euphoric quality, like an awakened dream. The illusion that Karen created was just as much a part of her as her smooth soft skin, her insinuating, provocative glances. To accept Karen without the illusion would be to reject her. Two irreconcilable tangents were the sum and substance of the whole. He wanted to absorb her completely.

"Don't keep staring at me, darling," she would always say.

He knew he had to have her, had to own her completely. He told her he was going to marry her. It was the night they went to the opera, Marilyn Horne in *Carmen*. Karen never looked more beautiful. Her black lace evening gown covered her shoulders fragilely, in an exciting contrast to her white skin. The diamond earrings he gave her shimmered as they caught the reflection of the spotlights onstage.

When the golden curtains at the Met closed on the final act he turned to her and said, "Tonight I'm going to take you to my home."

They drank brandy in front of his fireplace and the mellow embers flamed through the snifters, turning the liquor to gold. He put his arms around her and drew her slowly to him. She responded smoothly, easily. He kissed her gently at first. Then the embrace became almost suffocating in its intensity.

He knew as long as he lived he would never have enough of her. All at once he knew something else. It was incomplete. She didn't give any of herself. It was to have and to have not. She was the perfumed sables; she was the personification of loneliness. Yes, loneliness had come to life. Fate had played a cruel trick on him. Loneliness materialized in flesh and he was helpless to resist her. He knew, even that night, that Karen would sleep in his bed as long as forever was, yet would give him nothing of herself in return. It was a battle he would never win. He could sleep with her, take every part of her he wanted, yet he would never be able to satisfy her. Was this then the goal of his endless search? The invincible. Was that what he really was looking for after all? Karen became an exquisite torture he never wanted to do without. Did it matter if this secret obsession would ultimately destroy him? No one, not even himself, could understand the power of weakness, his special unique brand of weakness that he had always fought so desperately. But it was futile. Ultimately he had to accept it. The reason was simple. He could not live without it.

He was willing to pay the price, any price, to have her. They were married a few days later. He remembered the startled looks on the faces of people he knew. He could imagine what they were thinking, saying. It wouldn't last the year out. She was twenty-four. He was forty. She had no background, no education. She was merely a showpiece. Something for display, not for marriage. Something to admire. Not to love.

The marriage did last the year. It lasted eight whole years. It lasted until the night of May 10, almost five months ago.

No one would ever know what really happened that night except himself. He knew the questions that were formed on everyone's lips, all who knew her. But they were questions no one would dare ask. They were questions he would never answer. There was no notoriety. Just a brief item in the newspapers reporting the suicide. His whole battalion of publicity men saw to that. The Hewlitt name with all its prestige remained untouched, unscathed, just as before.

Memory is a strange equipment of the human mind. Every detail, every experience is stored up in memory. There is nothing the human mind can forget unless—it is blocked out by emotional compulsion.

He could not answer any questions now. He had blocked out the night of Karen's death completely.

Now all that was left was silence.

CHAPTER 7

John Chanin looked at his watch. If he could clear things up in a hurry today there might still be time to play nine holes.

He rang the buzzer on his desk for his secretary. "Anything urgent today, Mrs. Thompson?" She looked through the desk book she held in her hand. "No, sir. Just that Alan Prescott has been trying to see you."

"Prescott? Well, couldn't that wait until tomorrow?"

"I suppose so. But he's right outside. Shall I . . . ?"

"No, wait. Have him come in. I shouldn't imagine it would take long. Then call Marty Granger and ask him if he can meet me at the tenth hole at four."

"Yes, sir." He frowned as she left the room. If they lost the Hewlitt account it would take a sizable chunk out of billings, but what the hell, there was a competitor of Hewlitt's who might want to swing over to them.

John Chanin was feeling very good today. He was sixty years old, felt like fifty, and his golf handicap was just reduced over the weekend to an eight.

He tried to get hold of Mike Hewlitt when he received notice of the pending cancellation, but he wasn't available. Hewlitt was still pretty broken up about his wife's death. That was a weird thing, he thought. He remembered Karen Hewlitt fairly well. A beautiful woman, he recalled, but not exactly the right type for a guy like Hewlitt.

There was a knock on the door and Prescott walked into the room.

"Sit down, Alan." He motioned toward a chair near his desk. "What's on your mind?" he asked cordially.

Alan made a motion to loosen his collar, then thought better of it.

Chanin noticed the gesture. "Warm, isn't it? But you can't beat

Indian summer. As a matter of fact," he said genially, "I thought maybe I could get in nine holes today."

"I'll tell you, John," Alan said. "Jobwise . . . something's been bothering me." He coughed uncomfortably. He hated to use the advertising idiom, but it just slipped out. Jobwise he was getting hot under the collar. He was sure he was going to be gently eased out.

Chanin, too, mentally winced. "Shoot," he said with just a trace of irony in his voice. Chanin leaned back in his chair.

"It's about the Hewlitt account. I know what it means to the agency, the prestige . . ."

"Prestige, my ass," Chanin snapped. "Prestige hasn't got anything to do with it. It's a matter of cold cash."

Alan cleared his throat. "Well, that's what I wanted to talk to you about, John. It was my baby and it worries me a hell of a lot. I don't want you to think that I was responsible."

"What makes you think you're responsible? Are you?"

Alan shifted in his chair uncomfortably. "Not that I know of. But since his wife's death Mike went into some strange kind of seclusion. I tried to see him but . . . it was no dice. That is . . . I tried to see him on behalf of the agency."

"We haven't lost the account yet," Chanin reminded him.

"But if Hewlitt does resign the account, it sort of leaves me hanging out on a limb. What I mean is . . . I'd like some sort of reassignment."

Chanin broke into a hearty laugh. "First guy who ever asked me for more work. Got to hand it to you, Prescott. You're in there plugging all the time. Sure, we'll give you more work, if that's what you want. Why didn't you say so in the first place?" Chanin made a motion to lock up his desk.

Alan forced a smile, then got up from his chair. His hunch was right. Chanin was just a shade too buoyant, too jovial. They were going to ease him out if the account was lost. He was sure of it now. "Hear you shoot a top game of golf." Alan edged toward the door. "I'd like to take you on someday." He had to get through to Hewlitt somehow; and fast!

"Sure thing," Chanin called after him. He idly tapped his fingers on the desk. He heard Prescott had been playing around with Karen Hewlitt. Probably Mike found out. Well, he sighed. It was touch and go in this business. Clients canceled out for less reason than that. If they did lose the account, he knew he had two alternatives. He could forget about the whole thing and start wooing a replacement for the Hewlitt account. Better still, he could fire Alan Prescott and start working on Mike Hewlitt himself.

He looked out the window. What a day. He got up from his desk, grabbed his topcoat from the stand, and walked buoyantly out of his office.

CHAPTER 8

Miss McAvity replaced the phone crisply in its cradle and stared thoughtfully at the reproduction of the Winslow Homer seascape hanging on the wall opposite her. She rarely had to think over any decision she made regarding Mike Hewlitt, or Hewlitt Enterprises, for that matter. She had been more than a fixture for the Hewlitt dynasty longer than anyone could remember.

But when she set up the private appointment with Alan Prescott on the phone just now, she wondered if she had done the right thing.

She had been well aware that Mr. Hewlitt had carefully avoided any connection with those who knew his late wife. Especially Alan Prescott. But Mr. Hewlitt could not forestall this complication forever. She resolutely pressed the button on her desk, then opened the heavily paneled door in front of her.

"Mr. Hewlitt," she said directly, "I just arranged an appointment with you to see Alan Prescott this evening at your home."

Mike Hewlitt looked up from the impressive stack of papers he was studying. A momentary flicker of astonishment on his face was quickly replaced by an impersonal "Yes?"

"If you wish me to cancel it, of course . . ." She left it in mid-air.

"Well . . ." He hesitated.

"Naturally," she said, "I considered it imperative. He said there was something very urgent that turned up."

He might as well face Prescott. After all, he reassured himself, what could Prescott possibly know? But if he didn't see Prescott he'd never find out. So there it was. Everything he wanted to avoid suddenly became unavoidable.

He thought that again when the oak doors opened to let Prescott into his study that same evening. Alan's hearty greeting rang out hollowly in the hushed atmosphere of the dim room.

"Well, Mike!" Alan greeted him enthusiastically as he crossed the room, while he thought to himself, Christ, Hewlitt looks like hell.

"Hello, Alan," Mike replied quietly, rising from the shadows to greet him. "Brandy?"

"Don't mind if I do." Alan sat down on the leather chair opposite the fireplace.

Mike rang for the butler and as the drinks were set up he said, "I understand there's something urgent you wanted to see me about."

Alan waited until the butler left the room, sipped the brandy, then decided to try the direct approach instead of easing into it sideways. "Yes, there is something urgent I think you ought to know. It's about . . ." He hesitated, then plunged into it. "It's about . . . Karen." As he said the name he inadvertently glanced up over the fireplace at the portrait of Karen. Suddenly Alan felt chilled and uncomfortable. He was sorry he had come. What was it about this room? He looked around again more carefully. Why does it seem as if she's still alive? At once he realized this room was kept just as she left it. The portrait. The books she read. He took a cigarette from the silver box on the table. Even the cigarettes she smoked. He lit one. It was gold-tipped. He inhaled the smoke. Turkish. He looked at Mike, then pressed out the cigarette uncomfortably, as if Mike could read his thoughts.

Mike's eyes were inscrutable. His voice was expressionless when he said again, "What did you wish to see me about?"

Alan leaned forward in his chair. "I wanted to tell you," he said awkwardly, "how sorry I was about . . . about everything that happened. It . . . it was a terrible thing." Why did his voice sound so shaky? Even his hands were shaking. He reached for another cigarette. "I tried to get in touch with you sooner, but . . ."

"I know," Mike said tonelessly. "But I've been out of touch recently. However, thank you for your sympathy."

There was a curious remoteness about Mike. As if he had drawn a curtain between them. Even here in his own home, in his own room, facing him, talking to him, Alan felt he was impossible to reach. What actually happened the night she died? Did Karen inadvertently say something about him to Mike?

Alan tried again. "I happened to come across someone I thought might interest you," he said.

Mike was watching him silently.

"Someone who knew Karen." Alan cleared his throat.

There was a flicker of response in Mike's eyes.

"She came a long way to see you. She read about what happened. About Karen"—he paused almost imperceptibly—"about the suicide."

Mike remained motionless.

"I think you ought to see her, Mike. I think her arrival should concern you," Alan said. "She crossed an ocean to . . . to probe into something that's finished. Doesn't that seem odd to you?"

"The only thing that's odd is why it should concern you," Mike said.

Alan felt his face redden. "I'm sorry. I can see that I'm an intruder here. I shouldn't have come."

"I'm the one to apologize," Mike said quickly. "Naturally it would concern you," he said. "You knew her very well."

Alan wondered if he imagined the undercurrent of sarcasm in Mike's voice. But Mike went on blandly, in the same remote way. "Many people knew Karen very well. I suppose they also are concerned. It was an inexplicable tragedy."

"We're old friends, Mike. Or, maybe now I should just say we've known each other a long time. That's why I'm here. I think you should know. She's asking a lot of questions. It might prove to be embarrassing," Alan said. "Especially if she went to the newspapers or the police. Wouldn't you at least like to see her?"

"I prefer not to see anything or anyone even remotely connected with Karen," Mike said. "That part of my life is finished," he went on quietly. "I don't care to discuss it. There's nothing more to be said."

"Wouldn't you even consider meeting her?"

"Most certainly not," Mike said coldly.

"I had hoped," Alan said awkwardly, "in spite of everything, that perhaps we could remain friends. Your friendship has meant a great deal to me."

There was a gleam of mockery in Mike's eyes. "You aren't by any chance referring to the Hewlitt account, are you?" he asked suddenly.

"Partly," Alan said frankly. He took a deep breath. Three windows in his office, a whole career hinged on what he was about to say. "There's talk around the agency that we might lose the account. You know what that means to me. There's also talk that I might be responsible for personal reasons. I don't like rumors and I don't like that kind of talk. I prefer to deal with things directly. If there's anything you have to say to me, if you feel in some way I'm to blame because of what's happened—then let's have it out now."

Mike's face was set in hard, thin lines. "What has happened is part of the past. What happens in the future . . ." He held up his hands. "Who knows about the future? A million things can happen. Things no one can figure. You know that as well as I. As for the account—I haven't made any definite plans yet one way or the other. As soon as any decision is made I'll get in touch with Chanin." He paused. "Thank you for coming tonight. And thank you again for your sympathy." Mike had terminated the interview.

The image of the three windows shattered into a million fragments as Alan picked up his coat and left the Hewlitt mansion.

CHAPTER 9

The carrousel went around and around in a swirl of orange and red and shining brass. The blaring music of the calliope mixed with the shrieks of laughter from delighted children bobbing up and down on the wooden horses. Edith watched them, smiling. It was the carrousel in Central Park—an oasis of childhood ecstasy nestled cozily among trees near the lake. It was still here. Maybe not the same one, but just as bright, just as shiny as the one she and Karen rode when they were kids.

She could see Karen now, her eyes wide with anticipation as they walked toward the sound of the music.

"If you can grab the brass ring," Edith whispered excitedly to Karen, "it means a freeee"—she extended the word into three syllables—"ride!"

Karen's red curls bobbed along with the rhythm and her cherubic face broke into a triumphant grin as she looked down at her sister on the smaller wooden animal. Edith caught the smile and turned her head away quickly in the other direction. Tears sprung into her eyes. She didn't care about the bigger horse. The small horse she was on rode just as jauntily, just as rhythmically. But Edith was on the inside. Karen had made sure of that. Now she could never get a brass ring. Never, never, never. The tears dropped slowly down her cheeks. The horses went faster and faster. They raced around, up and down, the red, green, orange, and black horses melted into an exciting streak of flaming color.

A breathless little boy interrupted her thoughts. "Mama! Mama! The man said I won a free ride!"

He bumped into Edith, then ran over to a woman standing beside her. About five or six years old, Edith thought. The same age as Karen was. Twenty-six years ago. Why do I keep remembering? Why do I keep looking for the same places? The park was Alan Prescott's idea. But she had suggested the carrousel.

Alan rang for his secretary. "I'm taking a long lunch today," he said to Pat. "Business conference. In case anyone asks." But he knew, of course, no one would ask. Pat knew it too. She smiled at him sympathetically.

The danger signals were on—the sudden lack of memos, the phone that stopped ringing, the meetings he wasn't asked to attend. It was never anything positive, always negative. A slow, steady chopping away of responsibilities. No one was ever fired directly. Not the top echelon. Just gently eased out. He simply would have less and less to do until one day he'd walk into his office and start reading *Variety* from cover to cover, then *Billboard*, then *Hollywood Reporter*. At first it would be boring, then uncomfortable, then embarrassing, then downright humiliating. The next step was resignation.

Another job, Alan thought. Maybe. There was always a pipeline through to every other agency in the business. They knew about him. The impending amputation of the Hewlitt account was timed to perfection by Mike Hewlitt with the death of Karen. Alan could vividly see the handwriting on the wall, the handwriting of Mike Hewlitt.

Was Mike Hewlitt subtly pointing the finger of suspicion at him to cover up his own guilty feelings? Could it really be possible that Hewlitt drove his wife to suicide? Anything was possible. Even murder. Alan knew that. Just the way he knew the Hewlitt marriage was made in hell, not in heaven. But who could say whether the house on Sixty-eighth Street was a genuine citadel of grief, or a stage set, a camouflage for the truth? And only the truth, Alan figured, could clear his own name, lift the murky fog of suspicion. It wasn't only the Hewlitt account that he was losing now . . . it was his whole career.

A fantastic idea suddenly loomed in front of him. It hovered gently on the periphery of his consciousness, then broke forth with crystal clarity. There was one way to get at the truth. What if he could somehow re-create the identical set of circumstances which preceded Karen's death? Alan grabbed his coat and left the office.

He crossed the Plaza square to the entrance of the park at Fifty-ninth Street, and walked rapidly toward the carrousel. He appreciatively eyed the young woman in a sleek black suit in front of the merry-go-round, before he recognized that it was Edith. He took her arm and she turned toward him, startled.

"I'm not late, am I?" he asked her.

"I forgot about the time. I was watching the children."

"Let's walk toward the Plaza. We can lunch there." He engineered her toward the path.

They sipped martinis in the Edwardian Room, then Alan said, "You were right about Karen. It doesn't add up."

"You saw Mike Hewlitt?"

"I was at his home a few evenings ago." He paused. "Did I say home? It's a mausoleum."

"What do you mean?"

"It was the first time I'd gone back since she died." Then he said slowly, "Everything was just the way she left it. We were in the library. Her books were there, her cigarettes. Even her favorite chair. Nothing was changed, nothing moved. Karen's portrait still hung over the fireplace. The whole atmosphere was very curious. Sort of expectant. It was just as if . . . as if she were still alive, about to walk into the room at any moment."

"How . . . awful. He must have loved her very much."

"Or hated her." He said the words quickly, with intensity.

"Hated her?" Edith's hand shook as she put the cocktail glass down.

Alan lowered his voice. "Do you know why I think he lives in that shrine? He's created a stage setting, a ghostly backdrop for her memory to convince himself and the world that this is a monument to love. He's got to believe he loved her. Otherwise he'd go to pieces."

"I don't follow you, Alan. I don't know what you mean."

"Think it over a minute. If he really loved her the memory would perpetuate itself . . . in his heart, in his mind. Why does he have to put on a full-scale production? Because he feels he drove her to suicide . . . probably with his insane jealousy . . . his accusations. He's trying to blot out her death. He's acting as if it never happened. You get the feeling when you walk in there that Karen is about to enter any second."

"But couldn't you talk to him? After all, you were a good friend of his."

"I just couldn't reach him. I couldn't get through to him. He hardly said anything. The room, the place . . . Mike . . . it all gave me the creeps. Then as I sat there wondering how I could make a tactful exit a sudden horrible idea occurred to me. Why does he do this? Why? There was only one answer. Only one logical answer. He's got to keep her alive because . . . he feels so guilty."

Edith swallowed hard and reached for a cigarette. She wanted to speak, but the words wouldn't come.

"I don't want to upset you," Alan said. "But we both want to know the truth."

He lit her cigarette and she drew on it nervously. "It sounds like a nightmare. But maybe this is just your impression of what happened."

"You're right, Edith. That's why I want to get your impression."

"You arranged an appointment for me?" She asked it eagerly.

"I tried," he said. "But I couldn't swing it."

She was obviously disappointed. "Then how can I ever meet him?"

"I'll think of something, I won't let you down. I'll get an idea!"

Silently he reviewed his appraisal of the girl sitting next to him. It wouldn't do to tell her the idea now. Step by step, that was the only way to proceed. One wrong move, one hasty decision and it would all collapse. Build slowly, that was the only way. Edith Weston was not one to act impulsively. Her personality was more like her sister's than he originally thought. He needed more time. He had to solidify his relationship with her to sell her his idea. Otherwise she wouldn't buy it.

"How long can you stay in New York?" Alan asked her.

"Four more weeks. Unless I can get an extension on my leave of absence."

"Look . . . why don't you get a job in New York?"

"I couldn't. Really." She shook her head.

"I'll get you a job. A friend of mine is an editor at *Tempo*. There's an opening for a fashion writer." He persisted.

"No, really." She smiled at him.

"You'd like it here." He said it intimately. "I'll help you like it here."

She laughed. "No, thanks. But I'll write to *La Mode* tonight."

"Don't write," he said. "Cable."

"Okay," she promised.

He motioned to the captain for a menu. Solidify the relationship . . . it would be a pleasure, he thought. Pure pleasure. His pulse quickened as he recalled the lovely slim legs, the lean hips. She seemed so simple, so naïve at first, but now he knew there was a complexity, an intensity that pounded away beneath her deceptively soft, appealing exterior.

"You get that extension," he said. "And I'll get that idea."

Edith Weston was a challenge, he thought. He liked challenges. They were stimulating. Then he ordered luncheon for two.

CHAPTER 10

She hoped Alan's purpose in taking her back to his apartment was not to make love to her. It seemed like forever before he phoned again, although it was just a few days. And now they had finished dinner at one of those ubiquitous French restaurants that never quite succeeded in approximating the Parisian bistros she knew so well.

Edith surmised the early part of the evening was a kind of preliminary, a preamble to the ultimate proposition. But this time she was wrong. His purpose was the same as hers. And there was a completely different kind of proposition.

He picked up the photograph of Karen that was on the table. "Just a few minor changes," he said slowly, "and you'd be a dead ringer for Karen." He placed the photograph back on the table and turned to her. "How much longer can you stay in New York?"

"Two months," she said, pulling the cable from *La Mode* out of her bag. "I dared not ask for more."

"Two months," he repeated thoughtfully. "That ought to be time enough."

"To meet Mike Hewlitt?"

"You're going to meet him, all right," Alan replied quickly.

Her heart was pounding.

"I've been thinking about this for days," he went on. "I finally have it figured. I know how Karen died."

"You . . . know?" Edith could barely utter the question.

"She was poisoned."

"Not suicide, Edith. The reason Hewlitt feels so guilty is not because he drove her to suicide. It's because he killed her himself!"

She turned her head away. Suddenly she couldn't bear to hear the truth . . . have her suspicions turn to painful reality.

"It was made to look like suicide." Alan paced the floor. "I was at the coroner's inquest. They found traces of poison in her body . . . sodium thiosulfate."

She stared at him in silence.

"It's a deadly poison," Alan went on. "Anyone can buy it at a drugstore or a camera shop. It's called 'hypo'—a chemical used by professional and amateur photographers. It's a colorless liquid. There's no odor, no taste when it's mixed with brandy or a liqueur." He stopped in front of her. "Edith . . . one drink and that's it."

"But who bought the hypo?" she managed to ask.

"Karen did, at their corner drugstore. The day before she died."

"That proves it was suicide," Edith said, "doesn't it?"

"Karen didn't know anything about photography—but Mike Hewlitt did. It's a hobby of his. That's something Lieutenant Gerard doesn't know." He paused, remembering. "I saw thousands of dollars' worth of photo equipment in his home, including hypo. Mike was clever. I think he had Karen buy the hypo for him so the druggist could witness the fact and testify at the inquest. His plan worked."

Alan sat down next to her. "Karen was poisoned," he said again in measured words. "Murdered."

For an instant Edith looked as if she suddenly saw the truth and wished that she had never seen it. "Do you realize what you're saying, Alan? You're accusing someone of murder! How can you be so sure? You need proof. How are you going to get it?"

"I can't prove it," he replied. "But you can."

"You . . . you expect me to get some sort of evidence?" She stumbled on the words. Suddenly she felt afraid, as if she were hanging on the edge of disaster. One wrong step and she would plunge downward into oblivion. "The police have all the evidence," she protested numbly, "and it definitely pointed to suicide."

"We need evidence, but not the kind you think," he went on. "You're going to meet Mike Hewlitt by accident. A carefully pre-arranged accident. It's going to be a setup to prove murder."

"How . . . how can I?" Her voice was incredulous.

"You're going to re-create a phase of Mike Hewlitt's life . . . a series of circumstances that compelled him to kill."

"What are you talking about?"

"Patterns. Every human being has his own emotional pattern. He acts in a certain way to a certain set of prescribed circumstances. His emotional reactions are consistently responsive to certain stimuli, certain people. Give a person those stimuli and he'll react the same way to them as he's always done." He paused, and the words flowed with an eerie sound. "You are going to re-create a phase of Mike Hewlitt's life with his wife. You are going to become another Karen Hewlitt."

Edith stared at him, stunned. "That's . . . impossible. I couldn't. I wouldn't. The idea is fantastic! You don't realize what you're saying."

"You can do it. You must do it. Just a few minor changes . . . the color of your hair . . . the way you turn your head. I'll show you. I'll make you into another Karen. I'll arrange to have him see you somewhere, somehow. I'll show you how she walked, talked."

"I never could be Karen," she said hollowly.

"But you could look enough like her, act enough like her to make the wheels start spinning. Then just play him along. Get him involved enough to talk. How can you miss? The same face, the same figure. When Mike Hewlitt looks at you he'll be looking at Karen."

"But we have no right . . ."

"Just remember one thing. Karen had no right to die."

"No." She was trembling. "No, Alan. I can't do it. I won't."

"Please. Don't be upset. It isn't as fantastic or as difficult as you think." He put his arm around her. Then he took her face in his hands. "Just think about the idea. Think it over. There's nothing to worry about." He leaned closer and kissed her on her warm, pliable lips. "You're lovely," he said huskily.

She pulled away. She knew it was wrong. All wrong. The whole idea. Still . . . she wanted to meet Mike Hewlitt. Above all she must meet Mike Hewlitt. Maybe she could just go along with Alan's idea to a point. Just to meet Mike. Maybe if he saw her, the resemblance to Karen would be enough to get him initially interested. Then she could find out for herself about Karen. She wouldn't have to get involved with him. There would be no need to carry it that far.

"All you need is a little time to think it over," he said again, his arm resting around her shoulders.

She turned to him suddenly. "But why would he poison her? What was his reason . . . his motive?"

For a long moment he didn't reply. Then he said, "That night, just before she died, I spoke to her on the phone. She was upset, overwrought. I think he suspected she was playing around. He was insanely jealous. But he wouldn't give her a divorce. There must have been a raging argument that night."

"Was he jealous of you, Alan?"

"He was jealous of every man who looked at her." He said it evasively. He hadn't answered her question.

"You . . . you loved her," she said softly. This time it wasn't a question. It was a simple declarative statement.

"You said that once before and I told you: I was just a . . . friend."

"You loved her," Edith said again.

"You're so much like her," he murmured. "When all this is over maybe you and I . . ." He took her in his arms again, pressed his mouth against hers, and this time she responded. Her kiss was warm and passionate. Alan knew he had won. His Galatea was coming to life.

CHAPTER 11

She felt better when she saw him sitting solidly behind his desk. Of course, Lieutenant Gerard wasn't much help the first time. All he did was nearly frighten her to death. But Alan's idea of becoming another Karen plunged her into an emotional whirlpool. Karen was the vortex. The idea was both repellent and intriguing. But she had to reject it. There must be an easier way to get to Mike Hewlitt. And maybe Gerard knew it.

He pulled out a chair and offered her a cigarette. "I thought you'd be in Paris by now, Miss Weston," he said, holding the flame to the tip. "But anyway, I'm glad to see you're still alive and healthy." He shook out the match and ambled back to his desk.

She caught the innuendo in the bantering remark and looked at him quickly, but the smile remained set on his face.

Then Gerard said, "What's on your mind this time, Miss Weston?"

"There's been no sound of footsteps on silent streets," she said, "no strange face peering at me from darkened windows, no lethal poison in my martinis, no sleek black car trying to run me over. It's very disappointing, Lieutenant Gerard." Edith smiled.

Gerard didn't return her smile. Instead, he said, "When are you leaving?"

"Still trying to railroad me out of New York, aren't you?"

"A plane would be faster."

"I haven't even seen Karen's husband," Edith said, ignoring the suggestion. "So I cabled *La Mode* to extend my leave." She paused. "Lieutenant Gerard, I have to meet Mike Hewlitt. Couldn't you arrange it?"

"That again?" He shook his head. "I'm sorry, Miss Weston . . . that's impossible. Why can't you just accept the facts?"

"I wish to God I could," she answered in a low voice. "But how can I when it all points to . . ." She stopped.

"Murder?" Gerard supplied the word.

An ominous feeling crept over her. It seemed to be an unspoken warning, a warning that could only be felt, not heard. She wondered if Gerard too was experiencing this strange sensation. All at once she felt that Gerard could be right. She should take the next plane back to Paris. She should get away from New York before it was too late, but something was holding her back. What was it that rooted her here? The memory of Karen? The question of suicide? Maybe the answer would cost her her life. She shuddered.

"Miss Weston," Gerard was saying, "are you ill? Can I get you a glass of water or something?"

She shook her head. "I'm all right. It's just so close in here."

Gerard raised the window a few inches and some cooling air filtered into the room. "I'm afraid I made a mistake," he said with concern, sitting down behind the desk again. "The last time you were here I told you about a hunch. That was off the record. I was sure you understood. My official position is that your sister committed suicide. We can't play around with hunches," he said steadily.

Edith nodded mutely. Then she said, "We're not the only ones. I met Alan Prescott and he joined our little club. He saw Mike Hewlitt. He said his home looks like a . . . a mausoleum. A stage set to make people believe that it's a monument to her memory. A citadel to negate his guilt."

Gerard looked at her curiously. "We have no jurisdiction over the way people think. Or the way anyone is compelled to portray grief."

"But it's all so suspicious. The letter . . . the Iron Curtain that Mike Hewlitt rang down over his whole life. Nothing adds up."

"Miss Weston," Gerard said with finality, "I think you should skip the arithmetic, the speculations, and the suspicions. Let it alone. We can't help you. There's nothing you can do. Return to Paris."

Edith rose from the chair and started slowly toward the door. If only it didn't all seem so useless.

"Miss Weston," Gerard called out.

Edith stopped and turned toward him.

"Miss Weston, just one question," he said.

"What is it, Lieutenant?"

He said the words slowly, emphatically. "What made you cross an ocean to find out about a sister you never saw or spoke to in ten years?"

It was a simple question. But the words hit her with a sudden emotional impact that stunned her. The question was loaded. And she wasn't prepared for it. She had never allowed it to enter her consciousness. Gerard, in one sentence, had pulled the camouflage off the very core, the very essence of the free-floating menace, and let it lie there exposed, naked, frightening. But what was it, what form, what shape did it have? What name did it answer to? Some other time, perhaps, she could meet it face to face. But not now. She grasped the table near the door for the support she suddenly needed. Now she was too tired. It was too much.

Edith composed herself. Then she managed to smile. "You're right," she said. "I haven't got the answer for that one." She opened the door. "Goodbye, Lieutenant Gerard."

"Goodbye, Miss Weston," he responded pleasantly.

She nodded and left the office rapidly.

That night as Edith lay in bed, tossing and turning in the hollow silence of her lonely hotel room, she tried to find the answer to Gerard's question. She might have said Karen was her sister. It was her responsibility. There were a dozen answers to the question, she thought. But she knew none was the real answer.

She arose from the bed and went to the window. The cool air caressed her face. She could see the trees outlined in charcoal gray against the shadowy backdrop of early morning.

For a long time she sat there watching headlights pinpoint moving cars as they circled through Central Park. She wondered where they were going at this hour. Maybe to a house in the suburbs after an evening on the town. She felt a pang of loneliness. She couldn't possibly imagine what it was like, she who never had husband, child, home, family. Her life was completely apart, single and singular.

There was nothing I ever owned, she thought suddenly. Nothing to which I ever belonged, nothing that ever belonged to me. She was always on the outside looking in, the orphan child at Christmastime with nose pressed against the windowpane, viewing with wonder the glorious delights inside, just beyond her reach. If only she could reset the pattern, start all over again. Maybe it would be different. But it would never be different as long as she remained what she now was. And now she was only something that Karen created by her death. A wandering unknown person caught in the ebb and flow of time and space, seeking for she knew not what, reaching for solutions that possibly did not exist, ripping apart a maze of unknown quantities that became nebulous shreds in her fingers. Must this go on until she herself was ripped apart?

Maybe with the solution of Karen's death would come the answer, the final enlightenment, and then she could breathe again with freedom. The glass encasing the spectrum of life's glorious delights would shatter, and finally for the first time in her life she would be able to touch them, hold them, own them. Maybe then she would belong and belong to, and in this mutual ownership could she finally realize the fulfillment of identity. There was only one way left to solve the question of suicide. She had to become the replacement for Karen.

CHAPTER 12

The face that stared back at her in the mirror seemed strangely different. Edith ran a comb through her newly tinted hair. The light overhead gleamed on the bright auburn locks. Her skin was even whiter by contrast. She looked somehow older, more striking, more sophisticated. She even felt different, no longer plain and colorless, no longer uncertain and unsure. The first step had been taken. It was easy.

Alan's obvious admiration when he saw her that evening gave her confidence even more impetus.

"Perfect," he said. "It's just perfect. Mind if I let out a long low whistle?"

"I guess gentlemen prefer redheads," she said.

"I just prefer you," he replied. "We'll have to change the hair comb, though. Do you mind?" They stood in front of the mirror. "This isn't quite right." He pulled her hair back more severely from her face. He appraised her critically. A few soft curls fell casually on her forehead.

"There. That's a lot better."

She turned away from the mirror. "I feel like a fraud."

"You look like an angel."

"Like Karen?" Her voice was tremulous.

"It's pretty close. Now turn your head and tilt your chin up. The way she held her head . . . it was a very special way. Proud . . . aloof. Now walk."

Edith moved gracefully around the room. "That's fine," he said. "Even the walk is the same."

She sat down next to him. "I'm still not used to the idea," she said. "I wonder . . . Alan. I wonder what Karen was really like. What she really wanted."

"You're going to find out," he said. "Emotionally, even physically, you're going to live Karen's life from the first night she met Mike Hewlitt."

Edith's pulse quickened. Her hand tightened on the arm of the sofa. Karen's world was getting closer. "But how am I going to meet him? You still haven't told me."

"At a cocktail party given by Elise and Bill Martin. One week from tonight."

"How do you know he'll be there? You said he was practically a recluse." She was beginning to vacillate. What should she say to him? How should she act? What if Mike Hewlitt guessed the truth?

"Everything is arranged," Alan went on. "He'll be there. The Martins are very good friends of mine. And his. It's for Mike's favorite charity. Elise spoke to him on the phone. He'll be there. And so will you."

"And you . . . ?"

"No. That wouldn't be advisable."

She walked around the room nervously. "I'm afraid, Alan. I'm afraid to go alone. Maybe he won't even notice me." She said it almost hopefully.

"He'll notice you."

"What should I say, what should I talk about?"

"Anything except who you really are."

"What if he suspects that I'm related to Karen? You did. Wouldn't he?"

"We'll have to take that chance. If he does, then admit it freely. If Karen told him she has a sister, naturally he'll realize your resemblance to her is more than coincidence. But you said that was unlikely. So the odds are with us. If he doesn't know about you, then he'll react more strongly. He won't be as cautious. The wheels will spin a little faster."

It was all happening too quickly. She felt as she did on the plane. She wanted to escape, run from the haunting nameless fear that was looming larger and larger on the horizon. But she knew she could never run because the fear moved with her, breathed with her, lived with her. There was no escape. There was no turning back now or ever.

Number 2 Sutton Place South. It was Thursday night about seven-thirty. And it was a time and a place she wished she could obliterate now and for all time. She regretted the fact that she had ever agreed to this, even wanted it. She was frightened and now self-conscious. She felt as if she were someone else. She felt as if she were moving in a dream that was beyond any place and any time.

As she rode up the elevator to the penthouse she prayed that Mike Hewlitt had not yet arrived. She needed a drink and she hoped she'd be able to get lost in the crowd. She had to fortify herself before she saw him. How would she know him?

Edith stepped out of the elevator onto the plush red carpet in the foyer. The front door was open, and a butler took her wrap. She didn't have to worry about immediate introductions. The crowd was enormous, spilling over into every corner of the vast and fabulous apartment. A panorama of noise, laughter, music, voices surged about her. She edged her way toward the gigantic mirrored bar that was set up along one wall of the living room. She felt a sudden sense of relief. No one would recognize her. No one would know she had arrived. Mike Hewlitt wouldn't know she even existed. There was nothing to worry about. She was never more alone in her life and at this moment it was exactly what she wanted. She had time, time to calm down, get hold of herself, and time to get a drink. Then she could leave unnoticed. She felt easier now.

"What would you like, miss?" the bartender asked her.

"Scotch, please. On the rocks."

She picked up the drink and started to look around the room.

It was like looking at a cross section of all the people she had ever known. It was a massive conglomeration of women in the extreme "la mode" or stark simplicity that was just as contrived. Well-dressed men, tall, short, young, old. She knew that she had seen some of their faces on television, in the movies, and in the newspapers. Voices rang loud and clear across the din and hubbub, dropping names that people would read about in tomorrow's gossip columns, names that had "arrived." They were all there, writers, producers, actors, and executives.

Every second she could feel the overwhelming pressure they exuded. No one let go for a moment. They were all selling—themselves and each other. No one was buying. They were all talking. No one was listening. There was a curious synthetic façade about the whole procedure. Someone handed her another drink. It was a big expensive production with the right stars, the right producers, the right costumes . . . and yet it didn't quite come off. It was overdone, overstated.

"You must be Edith Weston." A hard, artificial woman peered earnestly into her face. Edith turned around, startled. The woman wore a black gown. Her glittering diamonds competed with her shiny blond hair for attention.

"I'm Elise Martin," the woman said, and shook her hand limply. "You must be Edith because you're the only one here I never saw before."

"Yes. It was very nice of you to invite me," Edith said politely. "Alan Prescott . . ."

"Where is the dear boy?" Elise gushed. "I do so hope he'll be able to make it. He said something about having to be out of town. Are you sure you're having enough to drink? Wouldn't you like to meet any of these people? Everyone is here, you know . . ." She went on and on without a pause for breath.

"Everything is fine," Edith broke in. "You have a magnificent apartment."

"Thank you, dear. You know, you look terribly familiar. Are you sure we haven't . . . ?"

"Quite sure," Edith said quickly.

"You're a look-alike then. But I can't quite seem to remember. Oh, well. It doesn't really matter. You'll excuse me now, won't you? There are some people over there I just haven't got around to yet." Elise Martin drifted off into the crowd.

Edith needed some fresh air. She walked out to the terrace, where the view was breathtaking. The terrace seemed to be suspended over the East River. The dark rippling water below was studded with lights from tugboats. She could even see the shadowy outlines of buildings across the river in the darkness. She stayed there for a long time, enjoying this panorama much more than the one inside. Suddenly she felt uncomfortable, as if someone was watching her. She turned. A tall man was standing a few feet away, leaning over the railing just as she was.

"Quite a scene, isn't it?" he said in a low voice.

"That's just what I was thinking," she agreed pleasantly.

He walked over to her and looked at the river below. "Rather a contrast to the other one." He nodded toward the living room.

There was something about him that was different from the others. Edith noticed that he was a good-looking man but not in the conventional way. There was a quiescent, moody intensity about him that clouded his darkly handsome face, and constrained his low, masculine voice.

Edith smiled at him. She felt an instant rapport toward him, a kind of empathy that sometimes one can feel even for a complete stranger. She wondered about it. Had she ever known him before?

Then all at once she instinctively knew she was looking at Mike Hewlitt.

Maybe it was the way he kept staring at her, her face, her hair. She felt a sudden sense of panic. Was this to be the meeting? Was this the moment she had been dreading and hoping for at the same time?

"You know," he said, watching her, "I've seen that very same smile a thousand times before."

"Really?" She tried to make her voice sound light, casual.

"It's quite incredible," he said slowly.

"What do you mean?" A hundred fears flashed across her mind. Her heart was pounding too loud.

"Your smile, your face, the way you turn your head. It's quite incredible," he said again. "Are you part of that group in there?" He stopped. "What I mean is—do you belong to that?" Again he motioned toward the people inside.

"No," she replied.

"I didn't think so," he said quickly.

"I guess I really don't belong anywhere," she said.

"Then that makes two of us. I'm Mike Hewlitt."

She wondered what Karen would have said, how Karen would have reacted to him. She tried to imagine that she really was Karen standing there on the terrace, seeing him for the first time.

"I have a sensational idea," he went on. "What do you say we join forces and get away from it all?"

"I'll get my wrap."

"I'll go with you," he said. "I can't take a chance on losing you now." There was a serious undertone to the bantering remark. They moved slowly through the crowd. Edith found her fur stole and his arms rested just for a moment around her shoulders as he helped her with it. A thrill of electricity ran through her. It was unexpected.

She had met Mike Hewlitt at last. He had an intensity, a force, an impact she hadn't imagined. The way he looked at her, the way he spoke to her echoed back to a time long ago, a time half-forgotten, when Karen stood under a spotlight and glowed, and all who saw her became enchanted. All who saw her became possessed. Mike Hewlitt had belonged to Karen's world. And now he was drawing her into it, step by step.

They sat at a table in a small secluded bar glowing with candlelight. They sipped their drinks and chatted, but Mike was thinking about the girl next to him. The cloud of soft red hair . . . the way she walked and held her head . . . the smile that played against the full red lips . . . it was all Karen. He wanted to reach out and touch her, hold her close, to convince himself that this wasn't a dream.

"You know," he said, "I wasn't just making conversation when I first saw you on the terrace. You do look exactly like someone else."

"People are always telling me that," Edith said lightly.

He took a small picture from his wallet and handed it to Edith. She looked at it closely.

"There is sort of a resemblance. But you flatter me."

He replaced the picture in his wallet. "I never thought I would see the same face again," he said. "Do you believe in fate?"

Edith took a sip from her glass, then put it carefully down on the table. "Not really. The long arm of coincidence, maybe. But not fate. You know what I think?" She smiled.

"What?"

"This is just another plot of how male meets female. But you've given it a slightly new twist—the girl in the picture. What did you say her name was?"

"I didn't say. But her name was . . . Karen." He paused. "What's yours? You still haven't told me."

"Edith. Edith Weston." She could tell from his face that he had never heard the name before. And for that she was thankful. Perhaps later, much later, she would explain about everything. But not now.

Mike took her hand. "I know a lot about you, Edith." Her heart skipped a beat.

"You must be psychic," she managed to say.

"Not really. But you interest me. And people who interest me have a curious effect. I'm never satisfied with surface impressions. I always go deeper," he said. "To find out if I'm right."

"And are you always right?" she asked, curious.

"Most of the time," he said. "Would you like a thumbnail analysis of Edith Weston?"

"Go ahead," she replied.

"I know that you're not married. Or at least . . . not working at it. But that's easy. No rings."

"What else?"

"I know that you have lived in Europe. Maybe studied there." He laughed at the startled expression on her face. "That's easy, too.

The way you talk. There's just a slight inflection. French, perhaps. Shall I go on?"

"Yes. You're amazing."

"You're in the fashion field. A model, maybe. The way you dress. You have a distinctive flair. A certain chic. Money alone can never achieve it. It's a style sense." He paused. "And you probably live alone. An apartment somewhere in the East Fifties. Stop me if I'm wrong."

"That's pretty close," she said. "Close enough."

"As for romance," he went on, "not at the moment. Otherwise you wouldn't be here."

Edith sat there in silence. She was stunned at his insight. Was it possible he knew who she really was? But still everything he said about her was all fairly obvious and logical. If he knew more, surely he would have told her. "And the story of your life, Mike?"

He paused a moment before he spoke. A deep, unfathomable expression crossed his face when he said, "I thought I might be able to write it over again. Maybe with someone like you. Maybe someone like you could give the last chapter a happy ending. I haven't given up hope yet."

"I've often felt that way," Edith said. "That I'd like to begin all over again. But . . . it's always too late."

Mike stared at the flickering candle. "As long as you live . . . there's still time. It's never too late. Always remember that."

"I'm sure," Edith said slowly, "that I'll never forget it."

"I have the feeling that I've known you from somewhere," he said. "Are you sure we never met before tonight?"

"I know we haven't."

"Maybe it's because of Karen," he said. "You look so much like her. You could almost have been sisters."

"Who is . . . Karen?"

"She was my wife. She's . . . dead."

For a long moment neither of them spoke.

"I'm . . . sorry," Edith said. And suddenly she was sorry, terribly sorry she had ever met him. Sorry that she was here.

She hated herself and Alan and the whole fantastic idea. If I could only run away . . . anywhere. But it was too late. It was always too late to turn back. She had to get hold of herself, keep going on and on with this fraudulent self she had become. Where would it end? The only answer she could think of was disaster, destruction. Why can't the end be now, right now? She had a wild desire to tell this man about everything. But something held her back. She was afraid. Afraid to hurt him, afraid to hurt herself. He isn't a murderer. He can't be. But what about Karen? She must find out. It was too late now.

He was going on about Karen. "It was a great shock," he said. "So sudden."

Edith felt numb inside. She could only listen.

"She had her portrait painted before she died. It's in my library. Every time I see it, I can almost hear her breathe. It looks so real I can almost feel the skin. Karen was a beautiful woman." He stared at the table, remembering. Then he said, "I would like you to see that painting. It could almost be a portrait of you."

"I'd very much like to see it . . . someday."

"Soon, very soon," he said urgently.

"No. I mean . . . you were right. I am living in France. Paris. I'm just here on a visit." The words stumbled out. "I won't have time. I have to go back. I have a job there. I'm a fashion editor for a French magazine."

Mike looked at her carefully. "What are you so afraid of?"

"Afraid? I don't know what you mean?"

"Don't run away, Edith. I won't let you."

"Why do you say that?" Her voice was rising nervously, out of control. "We're complete strangers."

He sounded calm and assured. "There's something more between us than just a casual drink. We both know that. You don't have to be afraid. What are you trying to run away from?"

"Nothing. Nothing." She fingered her glass tensely.

"I want to know more about you. I must see you again."

"I told you . . ."

"I know what you said. But your eyes are saying something else. We will see each other again. And again. We both know that too."

There was an urgency in his voice she couldn't ignore because she herself felt the same urgency. He was right. There was something between them. She felt completely helpless in this man's presence. He was like a magnet. Edith was trapped. She was frightened by her own emotions. But even greater than the fear was the fascination. She knew just as sure as she was sitting there that she would see him again. And again. And again. She had the strange sensation that she had lost herself, that Edith Weston no longer existed. Step by step she was moving into a strange new world. Mike Hewlitt made her feel as if she were Karen.

CHAPTER 13

Mike Hewlitt slowly walked up the massive circular staircase that led to the second floor of his home. Lately, he was finding it increasingly difficult to deal with even the most simple problems. Suddenly everything seemed to be endlessly complex. Each day a new inroad was made on his retreat into solitude. The closed door would not stay shut.

He reached the landing, started toward his bedroom, then stopped. Just a few steps beyond there was another door. A door that had remained locked for six months. Something compelled him to move on, beyond his room toward the closed door that was bolted upon a thousand tortured memories. He stood there motionless.

Then he placed his hand on the knob. The key was in his pocket. Just one turn of the lock and the door would open. He stared at the shiny brass knob like a man hypnotized. Then he glanced over his shoulder furtively. No one else was in the corridor. The servants had already gone to sleep. It was late. No one would know.

Quickly, he inserted the key, turned the knob. The door swung open, and he stepped inside, closing it after him, into the darkness.

The faint smell of her perfume still lingered in the air, musky now, imprisoned by the closed windows. He turned on the light. Everything in the room was of a delicate ivory hue—the luxurious satin curtains, the coverlet on the bed, the velvet chairs, the soft carpeting, the antique chandelier overhead.

A book was resting on the night table, held open by her reading glasses. He walked closer to the bed. The pillow, the spread were still creased by the outline of a body, her body.

He walked to the closet and swung the doors open. There were dozens of gowns, gossamer chiffon, gleaming satin. There was the yellow satin gown she wore when she sat for her portrait. He fingered it gently. His hands ran over the smooth satin. It felt like her skin. He touched the luxurious furs . . . the sables he had given her for Christmas. He remembered her smile of delight when she opened the white package tied up with masses of red ribbons.

He moved as in a trance to the small writing table. There was a telephone, a pad, a pencil. He picked up the white leather appointment book and thumbed through the dated pages. Her thin light handwriting had recorded luncheon engagements, theater parties, beauty-salon appointments on the various pages.

Then his eyes were held on the initialed notation that was carefully marked on a back page dated December 25. Christmas Day. "E.W." That was all. Just "E.W." He stared at the page for a long time, thinking.

He could see her sitting at her desk as she penciled in those two initials, as she used the telephone, as she sat and spoke to him. Her voice was low, melodic. Carefully controlled, confident, smooth—like satin. He could see her delicate long fingers reaching for a cigarette, the special imported Turkish kind, and placing the gold tip gently into her red full lips. He was a man possessed in her presence. Even in this room, even now, he was possessed. He could see her move, walk, breathe. It was as if she was here with him in this room.

He started to tremble. He sat down at the small writing table and his hands gripped the edge until the knuckles became white. The memories were so vivid, so real, so painfully alive. So alive that they were no longer memories. The past had become the present.

"My God," he murmured, and put his head down on the desk in his arms. His body started to shake. Then suddenly low, racking sobs heaved his body, tortured sounds, so tortured they were almost inhuman.

Finally the sounds were quiet, the shaking stopped. He lifted his head and listened, as if the sounds came from some other place, not inside himself.

The room was quiet, still. No wind brushed the heavy draperies, no voice filled the emptiness, no footsteps trod upon the carpet. It was a still, silent room. It was a room of death.

He picked up the appointment book again and fingered the pages. There was a time long ago when he thought his lifetime could be like this. A calendar of dates. He thought he would be able to rip out and cast aside the pages of yesterdays. Today would be the only focal point of his life. The tomorrows were pages waiting to be filled. But it was becoming increasingly impossible to make the transition from the yesterdays. Places, things, people began to sharpen the painful memories.

December 25. "E.W."

Edith Weston. The same face. The same voice. The same hair. The way she walked. If he couldn't remember a certain detail of her face . . . he just had to walk into the library and look at the portrait. What did she want? Who was she? Why had she suddenly appeared in his life?

He should have known, guessed. It was more than coincidence. He did know.

He knew from the first when he stood on the terrace at the Martins' cocktail party and watched her, the way she moved, the way she held her head. He noticed that her hair was tinted the exact shade of red as Karen's. Why? Karen's past was immersed somewhere beyond reach. His wife had no parents, no relatives. She told him she was an orphan. He knew a little about her first marriage. He asked nothing more.

Could it be that Edith Weston was related to Karen? How much did she know? What did she suspect? Why had Karen never mentioned her? Why was Edith Weston just E.W. on an engagement calendar? He was suspicious even when he first saw her.

But Edith Weston fascinated him. It was like seeing the form of Karen with another soul. It was no use. He couldn't escape it. Karen in any form would always intrigue him. He would always pursue the fact, the form, and the fantasy. It was his nemesis.

He picked up the phone on the desk and dialed a number. Then before the connection was completed he hung up. Lieutenant Gerard of the Homicide Division would think it more than a little strange. A phone call from Mike Hewlitt after six months. A phone call to the police to check up on Edith Weston at this time of night. He stared at the ivory room. He must get hold of himself. He left the room quickly, locking the door. Tomorrow he would casually drop in at Gerard's office. After all, Gerard was most sympathetic at the inquest. Tomorrow. Just a friendly visit.

Gerard seemed very pleased to see him. But his bland manner didn't fool Mike for a second. It was a perfect façade calculated to disarm any antagonist.

"Well, Mr. Hewlitt," Gerard said benevolently, "what can we do for you today?"

"I'll get right to the point, Lieutenant Gerard." Mike leaned forward in the worn leather chair opposite the desk. "I was just wondering if anywhere in your investigation you happened to discover that my wife had any relatives."

"I should think you'd know better than we do, Mr. Hewlitt."

"My wife was very reticent about her past."

"I see." Gerard got up from his desk and walked over to a cabinet marked "Inactive Files." He leafed through the folders and pulled one out. "I really ought to move this over to our active files," he said.

Mike looked at him sharply. "What do you mean?"

Gerard ambled back to his desk with the folder in his hand. "Nothing special." Gerard had picked up a square white envelope from the folder and was turning it over in his hands. "Yes, your wife had a sister," Gerard said, and looked over at Mike. Mike's face was expressionless.

"She's been living in Paris," Gerard continued, "for the past ten years."

"A sister who lived in Paris." Mike kept his voice steady, flat.

"Yes." Gerard replaced the envelope in the folder. He glanced at Mike questioningly.

"I see." Mike's fingers beat out a rhythmic tapping on the arm of the chair. The tapping stopped. He folded his hands.

"Lieutenant Gerard," he said after a moment, "who is Edith Weston?"

"So that's why you're here," Gerard said.

Mike nodded.

"That's what I assumed."

"You still haven't answered my question."

"Don't you know who Edith Weston is? You've seen her, haven't you?"

"Yes, I've seen her," Mike said.

"That alone is answer enough, isn't it?"

"My wife's maiden name was De Witt. Not Weston," he said.

"I know. She had changed it legally about twelve years ago. From Weston to De Witt." Gerard tapped the folder. "We discovered that when we checked up on Edith Weston."

"What does she want?"

"To find out what happened. Naturally."

"I thought this case was closed," Mike said tightly.

"Death in itself is a form of finality, Mr. Hewlitt," Gerard replied, "but it's an end that causes many beginnings. It's a power that can uncover true feelings . . . hate, lust, greed, love. Death brings out the basic emotions in those who remain and starts new complications. Life and death." He spread his strong thick hands on the desk. "This is our business. We are familiar with many of the consequences of both."

Mike listened as Gerard spoke. But he heard only words strung together. He was seeing two initials on the page marked December 25—E.W. "Does anybody else know about this?" Mike's face was strained. The tension broke through into his voice.

"Take it easy, Mr. Hewlitt," Gerard said gently.

"Isn't there a law to protect a man's privacy?" Mike asked.

"There's nothing illegal about Edith Weston's desire to find out what happened. It's natural, isn't it?" Gerard looked at him curiously.

"She didn't tell me she was Karen's sister."

"Maybe she had reasons."

Mike's eyes were riveted on the folder. "Who else knows about Edith Weston?" he asked.

"Just a"—Gerard hesitated slightly—"a friend of yours," he said. "Alan Prescott."

Mike rose from the chair. His face was hard, impregnable. "So that was the person he wanted me to meet," he said slowly. But he was thinking fast. Prescott must be using Edith Weston to probe the suicide verdict. Probably a form of blackmail to insure the Hewlitt account.

Gerard looked at him quizzically.

"Alan Prescott." Mike repeated the name. "I wasn't aware that they knew each other." He moved toward the door. "Well, thank you very much, Gerard. You've been very helpful." He would have to act fast now. Prescott was suspicious. Maybe he knew what happened. There was one way to stop Prescott. Reinstate the account. The power of money was without peer.

"I hope so, Mr. Hewlitt," Gerard replied. "I most certainly hope so."

"I guess that explains Edith Weston," Mike said, his eyes still on the desk. But he wanted more explanation. And he wanted it straight from Edith Weston. He wondered how far she intended to go with her little research project.

Gerard didn't answer. His eyes followed Mike's to the folder on the desk. For just an instant there was a curious oblique expression on Gerard's face that was quickly replaced by obsequious courtesy. "Just call on me anytime at all," he said. "Anytime."

Mike caught the transition. He kept his hand on the doorknob. "I'll do that," he said. Then he left quickly.

Gerard picked up the manila folder again, took out the letter, and opened it. He sat there for a long time regarding it with a puzzled expression on his face. He rubbed his chin thoughtfully. Then he lifted the receiver of his phone from the cradle.

"McGehee? Get me the complete transcript of the Hewlitt inquest, will you?" he said into the phone. "Karen Hewlitt, this past May." He paused with the receiver to his ear. "And I want a check made on all major airline and boat reservations to Paris arriving on or just before December twenty-fifth." He paused again. "That's right. From New York to Paris, or it could be to Le Havre or Cherbourg. Put two men on this. It might take quite a bit of time." He gently replaced the receiver.

CHAPTER 14

Saturday evening. It was the opening night of a big Broadway musical. It was just two nights after the Martins' cocktail party and Mike Hewlitt had phoned the very next day. Their first meeting was too fraught with her own apprehensions to make any sense. She only knew she had to see him again.

The music from the orchestra pit blended with the murmur of the mink and limousine audience as they crushed toward the exit doors of the theater to get a smoke during intermission. But Mike made no move to leave.

"I hate crowds," he said to Edith. "Do you mind if we remain here?"

"Not at all," she said.

The theater was jammed with celebrities, newspaper critics, and the regular array of first-nighters.

"How do you like it?" he asked her.

"It's a wonderful show," she answered politely. But she was waiting for the final curtain to drop. Maybe tonight . . . tonight she would find out about Karen.

The warning bell for the second act sounded and the crowds started moving back toward their seats. The lights dimmed and the curtain went up.

Edith was looking at the stage but she was thinking about the man sitting next to her. The first time they met she supposed he was at least fifty years old. He was a tall, handsome man whom some would call formidable. He had graying dark hair, deep lines in his face, and an ironclad reserve that instantly set him apart from all others. Still, more acute observers would sense a kind of caved-in emotional intensity, a passionate urgency about him that lurked just beyond the surface. He was difficult to know. He was mystifying, intriguing, and at times completely charming. Yet he conveyed something else, still another impression that was less defin-

64 *Living Image*

able, more frightening. In Mike Hewlitt she sensed danger from the start.

She had accumulated so much fear in her thoughts about him that he had become someone unreal. Someone who had a name but whom nobody really knew. She wished that these few hours in the darkened theater ablaze only with footlights onstage could go on forever. As long as she was in the audience and as long as Mike Hewlitt remained in the dark—she was safe. Her fantasies about him and what happened to Karen were frightening. But they were only fantasies. And the fears . . . just stage fright. But when the curtain would ring down on the final scene and the lights would go up in the audience, she would have to face reality. A reality that could be terrifying!

The Hewlitt limousine was waiting for them in front of the theater. The motor purred softly as they drove off. The traffic seemed to part just for them. Mike told the chauffeur to head downtown.

"Do you remember Greenwich Village?" he asked her.

They were touring through the offbeat streets now with the myriad shops and walk-ups clumped together into an odd zigzag pattern. There was nothing terrifying about this. Just Greenwich Village and the chauffeur in the front seat.

"Yes. There was a place I used to go. The Village Vanguard," Edith said, remembering the match cover Karen had pasted on the wall of their apartment a long time ago. Another world ago.

"It's still here," he was saying. "Certain sections of New York have personalities as individual as people."

She was wondering why he didn't take her to the usual aftertheater places, like Sardi's or Danney's. But then he had already told her he hated crowds. And he had successfully managed to avoid them all evening.

"I hope you don't mind," he said, "if we just take this tour on wheels."

"I don't mind at all," she said. "But I'm beginning to think you just don't like people."

He pulled out a cigarette and lit it for her. As she took it he reached for her other hand, and held it in his.

"What were you saying about people?" he asked her.

"It seems as if you have an aversion to them," she replied easily, reassured by their casual conversation.

"Oh, I have a whole list of hates," he said lightly. "People, public-

ity, smoky rooms, cocktail parties." Then he added, "And predatory women."

Edith felt her face flush in the dark.

"Are you a predatory woman?" The badinage had gone from his
voice.

"I . . . I don't know exactly what you mean," she said uneasily.

"Don't you? I thought it was self-explanatory. I mean the kind of
woman who wants something for nothing. Grasping, avaricious.
The kind of woman who will take everything and give nothing. But
then that kind usually has nothing to give."

"I'm sure you were never involved with anyone like that," she
said.

"What makes you so sure?"

"Because you seem to be so . . ." She groped unsteadily for the
right word. "So . . . careful. I mean"—she faltered—"you have so
much insight."

He laughed hollowly. "Anyone can be wrong. Even I."

They rode along in silence. Mike had released her hand and was
staring pensively out the window as if he were silently reappraising
her. She began to feel the free-floating menace hovering closer and
closer. The limousine had become a prison. She wanted to escape.
Instead, she reached out desperately for the impersonal.

"You must hate New York too. It's so overcrowded." She tried
limply to reactivate the former topic of conversation.

"It's a million little islands and each has a heartbeat," he replied.
"I like New York. It's a way of life with many facets of character."

She clung to the topic. "But you said you hated crowds. Surely
New York has even more than Paris."

"But this can be the loneliest place in the world. It depends on
what you're looking for. Excitement or loneliness. Here you can
have your choice." He spoke with renewed vigor.

She bit her lip and tried to approximate his fervor. "You're about
the best guide a tourist could have." But it came out all wrong.
Somewhat like a hoarse croak. It was the best she could do. Acting
wasn't in her line at all.

Then suddenly: "Are you really just here to see the sights?"

Her head spun around. Her face went white in the darkness. "Of
course," she managed to answer.

"Just a tourist," he said in an odd way.

"Just a tourist," she agreed lamely. She couldn't keep up with his abrupt transitions. The pace was too fast. He was much too keen for her. Too perceptive. Or was it still just her own capricious imagination?

"That's too bad," he said. "I thought perhaps you had found something interesting enough to make you prolong your stay. Maybe stay in New York for good."

"I have a job in Paris," she answered quickly.

"And you haven't thought about changing it." It wasn't even a question. It was an insistent challenge to admit the truth.

"I really haven't given it any thought at all." She tried to skim over it lightly.

But he wouldn't let it go at that. "Well, I have. And I was thinking maybe you did change your mind."

"Maybe I haven't found anything that interesting." The words just seemed to spill out.

"All the more reason to stay then, isn't it? You probably need more time."

Now the pounding of her heart was so strong there were no words at all. Just panic twisted around questions. How much did he know? He acted so strange. His questions were so odd. Yet . . . it was perfectly natural, wasn't it?

Mike leaned forward and gave the chauffeur the address of the Gotham Hotel. He turned to Edith and said almost apologetically, "It must be getting late."

She hadn't thought about the time. But now she looked at her watch. It was only twelve. It wasn't late at all. And wasn't it unusual not to suggest a drink before he brought her home? It was almost as if he were anxious for the evening to come to an end as rapidly as possible.

He escorted her through the lobby of the hotel to the elevator.

"I've had a lovely evening," she managed to murmur.

"Did you? I'm glad." He sounded so far away, so impersonal. So different from the first time they met.

She held out her hand and he shook it lightly.

"Goodbye, Edith." He turned and left abruptly.

That was all. Just goodbye. He was gone, out of sight, when she stepped into the waiting elevator.

She entered her nondescript hotel room and sat down on the small wing chair near the bed, her coat still around her shoulders. She sat there a long time wondering why everything went wrong.

His sudden dark moods, his cold probing questions . . . tonight was such a complete reversal of the man she first met at the cocktail party. Yes, Mike Hewlitt was a man to be feared. A dual personality. Paranoid? Wasn't that what Gerard said? They could be dealing with a paranoid.

She shuddered and drew her coat closer, and turned on the lamp. Even in the soft light the room looked transient. Just like her life. She couldn't stay here much longer. The room was getting on her nerves. Why didn't she leave and go back to Paris? She was trying to act out two lives at the same time, hers and Karen's, when she could barely struggle through one. But she knew she was caught in a current of emotions that was beyond her control. Her purpose, her goal was . . . Karen. She seemed so close to the truth now. She just needed more time. If she could only—stay in New York. Maybe get a job. Alan . . . once he even offered her a job. Well, why not? Why not get a job in New York? She reached for the phone eagerly.

It was almost as if Alan was waiting for her call. "Christ, you're getting elusive," he said. "I've been trying to reach you for two days."

"I didn't phone sooner because I've been waiting to give you the full report," she said.

He lowered his voice. "You've seen him, haven't you?"

"I've just left him," she said softly into the phone.

"No wonder you've been playing so hard to get," he said. "Need I ask? How did it go?"

"Fine—the first time. At the Martins' it was just what you expected. But tonight . . ." She paused, fingering the receiver.

"What's wrong?"

"Everything," she replied. "He was different. Rather I should say . . . indifferent. And strange. Almost as if he knew about me. I . . . I'm frightened, Alan. What if . . . if he . . . ?"

His short, alarmed whistle came over the wire. "Hold on now, Edith. Let's not get carried away. You're perfectly safe. The worst that can happen is that he'll fall in love with you," he said encouragingly.

"Sorry to let you down." She laughed uncomfortably. "I guess it's this room . . . this living alone and not liking it. It's depressing."

"You can always count on me, sweetie. Just reach for the phone. Even on Saturday night . . . here I am," he said cozily.

"That's what I was hoping," she said into the phone. "Because I need your help, Alan. You said something once about a job. Is it still open?"

"*Tempo* magazine? It sure is! And you're just the girl. Matter of fact, I was telling Maddy Phillips about you the other day."

"Do you know her well? I mean, could you set up an interview?"

"I'll set up the job! Maddy's a friend, a real old friend," he said pointedly. "Look, tomorrow is Sunday. I'll call her at home and you be over at *Tempo* early Monday morning."

"As easy as that?"

"After all, you're a Paris import, girl. How could Maddy do better?"

"And how can I ever repay you?"

"First, get the job. Phone me Monday at the office and let me know how it goes."

She could hear the click at the other end of the line. Just a click. But to her it was a sesame. She wanted to turn back the clock, reconstruct a lifetime. Now she really might have the chance—the time to find all the pieces of the jigsaw puzzle. She would find out what happened to Karen. Then she could live . . . a new career, new friends . . . her own apartment. It would be wonderful to live in New York. She stopped suddenly. As long as she lived, that is.

CHAPTER 15

Monday morning Alan found a memo from John Chanin on his desk and his secretary draped seductively against the doorway.

He read Pat first. Then he read the memo. That was an invitation too. To Chanin's office.

Pat drawled sweetly, "Tom Belding wants to see you also."

Almost simultaneously, as if on cue, Tom poked his head in the door. "Hi ya, fellow," he boomed. "What's with it?"

"Hear the Carter show went full network. Nice going, Tom." Alan tried to sound sincere. Belding had been avoiding him since they had that drink together three weeks ago. Belding's friendship or lack of it was a fairly accurate barometer as to how the wind was blowing.

Today Tom looked exuberant. "How about lunch, Alan? The fellows are going to the Oyster Bar at one."

Alan gave him the okay sign with his thumb and forefinger. Belding grinned and vanished.

"Looks like we're in business again," Alan said to Pat. He pressed her well-rounded shoulder. The skin felt soft under the tight black silk jersey blouse. He got the message. But he had a more important one to take care of at the moment. He had no idea why or how, but he knew as sure as he was sitting at his desk that he could again enjoy that three-window view from his office.

"I'll be in J.C.'s office," he said going out. "In case anyone calls . . ." he added. But this time his voice held no note of banter and she didn't deliver back one of her soulful looks. Like he said, they were in business again.

J.C. motioned for him to sit down. "About the Hewlitt account, Alan . . ."

Alan cleared his throat. Here it comes, he thought. For better or for worse. But it couldn't be for worse. Not after his quick séance with Belding. He relaxed and sat back against the soft green leather chair.

"I had a talk with Mike Hewlitt late Friday. Actually he called me about the account." Chanin paused. "You know Hewlitt is a pretty straight-shooting guy, so I asked him to lay it on the line. Especially since the general opinion was that there was perhaps some personal misunderstanding with you."

"Hewlitt and I never had any misunderstanding, John."

"Perhaps not. But there was talk." He broke off suddenly. "Well, never mind about that. Fortunately, Hewlitt didn't discuss the personal phase of it at all. He thought we were doing a fine job with the account."

"Then why, sir . . . ?"

"I'm getting to that. The reason Hewlitt wanted to close our billing was personal in a way. But it had nothing to do with you," he said. "Hewlitt was planning to retire."

"Retire?"

"I was just as surprised as you. He was going to liquidate the business. Sell out. Just between you and me, Prescott, I'm sure his wife's death was the cause of that. He took it very hard at first. But"—Chanin smiled at Alan—"but he's coming out of it. He sounded pretty good on the phone."

"At least he sounded," Alan said.

Chanin laughed. "He's certainly been a hard man to reach these last six months. But he's coming around. Our contract with them expires in two months, right?"

"Fifty-two days, John."

"He said we could start thinking about the new campaign and he'd give us a definite answer at the end of this month."

Alan sighed with relief. You could always count on Belding, the barometer, he thought. "That's just great, John."

Chanin smiled. "So we'll just sit tight." The phone on his desk started to ring. He nodded toward Alan in a gesture of dismissal.

It wasn't until Alan reached his own office that his feeling of euphoria dissipated. It was when he picked up the ringing phone on the desk and heard Edith's voice on the other end of the line.

"Alan," she said excitedly, "I've got the job! I start at *Tempo* next week."

He took a slow beat before he replied, "Fine, that's fine, Edith." Inside he shriveled. The whole thing could backfire now. All she had to do was get something on Hewlitt, any bit of damaging evidence, and the account would be pulled right out from under him.

"As soon as I said Paris and *La Mode* I had it made," Edith bubbled happily.

"I knew you'd connect, sweetie," Alan told her. "You couldn't miss." He couldn't unsell her about the job. There wasn't a chance. Edith Weston was here to stay. She wanted more time to reach Hewlitt and now she was going to get it. Thanks to the philanthropic organization named Alan Prescott. But maybe he could unsell Mike Hewlitt, somehow convince her to stay away from him. She said he seemed disinterested. That was at least a starting point.

"That calls for a celebration, doesn't it?" said Alan. He thought about her startling resemblance to Karen with her newly tinted red hair, and her firm, lithe body. "How about dinner tonight?"

"I'd love it," she replied.

"I'll pick you up about eight, okay?"

"Eight o'clock. Fine."

"See you for dinner, sweetie." He hung up the phone, whistling the theme song of the Carter show.

Right after dinner they went to his apartment. He fixed two drinks at the bar. "So you're all set at *Tempo*." He returned with her glass.

"Thanks, Alan." She held up the glass. "For the small favors and the big ones." She sipped her drink.

"Never mind the gratitude." He sat down next to her. "Now that you have a shiny new job, what's your next move?"

She laughed. "A shiny new apartment, I hope. And what's your next move?"

He kissed her lightly on the lips. "You're very attractive. Or did I tell you that before?"

She glanced at him provocatively. "So that's your next move?" The way she said it—it was warm and sultry—it was the way Karen would have said it.

He wanted to move in fast but he knew he would have to handle her with care. The time for talking still wasn't over. "Now that you're here to stay, sweetie . . . you can relax and enjoy it. You've got a whole new life ahead of you."

She shook her head. "Not quite . . . and not yet, Alan. Are you forgetting why I decided to stay?"

"Still thinking about Mike Hewlitt?" He said it with insouciance.

"About Karen," she corrected.

"I thought maybe you changed your mind after Saturday night. You said he was disinterested."

"Maybe he'll change his mind," she said. "He's a strange man. Completely different, unpredictable. I suppose Karen would have been attracted to someone like that. He has tremendous intensity. He's . . . well"—she groped for the right adjective—"she must have found him . . . magnetic."

"Sure you're not analyzing your own feelings?"

Edith looked at him with surprise. "What do you mean?"

"Just because you found him magnetic doesn't necessarily mean that Karen did."

"Any woman would."

"Now you're generalizing."

"What's the matter with you tonight, Alan?" There was a quick shift in his attitude. She couldn't figure it out. "You seem different. Not as enthused. Is there anything wrong?"

"It seems a pity to concentrate on a dark past when you've got such a bright future."

But she didn't accept that. "Now you're being evasive. What's wrong?"

"Why don't we forget Mike Hewlitt?"

"You're not serious?"

"Dead serious. Let's forget the whole idea," he said. "It was a foolhardy thing anyway."

Edith felt her face get hot. "Forget the whole idea? Forget about Karen? You suddenly get a crazy impulse to toss everything out the window, and I'm supposed to play along like a puppet! Don't you have any feelings at all?"

He pulled her closer to him and kissed her roughly on the mouth. "That's what my feelings are," he said huskily.

She pulled away. "Did you ever think about my feelings? You know how much this means to me. I'm not used to such sudden switches," she said with anger.

"This isn't sudden, Edith," he said. "I think what we planned is wrong, all wrong."

"When I said that the other night—you laughed at me."

"That was the other night," he replied. "This is tonight. Why waste a day, a minute digging up memories? You're trying to be Karen and that makes you a fraud, Edith. It won't work. You're living in the past. You're doing what he's doing. We're real, you and I. We're alive. The rest is dead . . . like Karen. Why don't you learn to live?"

Edith drew back. She felt as if he had slapped her across the face. "It was your idea to begin with. You said you would help me." Tears flooded her eyes. "You're the fraud. You were only leading up to this," she said furiously. "I don't know what you're up to now and I don't know why you're so anxious to stop me. But there's one thing I do know. You're too old to play games!"

He tried to talk to her. He tried to take her into his arms. He wanted to say something, anything. But she broke away and picked up her coat. Then she ran out the door, slamming it behind her.

Alan took the two empty glasses and set them back on top of the bar. He caught his own reflection in the oval mirror that hung on the wall over the walnut commode. He noted that his dark hair was receding even further. The thin, handsome face was beginning to show more furrowed lines around the mouth and at the corners of the steel-gray eyes. His haircut, which he always assumed gave him the mark of distinction that belonged to a Harvard man, now looked as if it belonged to another generation that definitely wasn't his. He was forty-seven, he felt like forty-seven, and now he finally looked like forty-seven. Edith Weston called his bluff. How much longer could he go on playing games? How much longer could he go on being the juvenile delinquent and get away with it? The face in the mirror glared back at him, mocking, accusing. "You jerk," he said, staring at it. "You dumb jerk!"

CHAPTER 16

Even in a business renowned for its snob appeal, *Tempo* was a fashion magazine conspicuous for its loftiness. It carried its proud head high on the twenty-second floor of the Squibb Building at Fifty-eighth Street and Fifth Avenue. From the slick receptionist's office, muted in shades of white, gray, and black, to the inner sanctums of the editorial staff, papered in vast panoramic scenes of Manhattan, *Tempo*'s shiny personality was self-consciously held aloof from the common level.

It was an accurately contrived mirror for the chic, high-styled women who set the pace in modes, manners, and morals for their less fortunate counterparts.

After a few days of frenzied activity, Edith slid into the comfortable niche of familiarity. Observation had quickly taught her that Madeline Phillips ran the show. Beneath Maddy's effusive, overwhelming exterior was a well-organized business acumen. But like so many who have a talent for business, Maddy had no talent for living. Her personal life was completely disorganized. It was a hopeless incongruity.

"Enjoy," she proclaimed over her third martini at lunch with Edith. "Enjoy and to hell with the rest of it. Why should I beat myself to a pulp worrying about some guy?" she demanded. "If someone comes along who's interesting—well, okay. And if not, that's okay too."

"What about your husband?" Edith asked her.

Maddy's angular face formed an expression of utter disbelief. "This girl is straight out of *Alice in Wonderland*."

Edith laughed. "He must be very tolerant."

"What do you suppose he's been doing these last six months in London?" She raised an eyebrow. "But we have what is known in the trade as an arrangement."

"I never thought arrangements worked."

"When Stan is here we're made for each other. When he isn't
. . ." Maddy shrugged her lean shoulders. "It's the way the ball
bounces. You ought to know, Edith. But stick around, you'll learn.
Like Alan said, you're a bright girl."

"That's some arrangement," Edith said.

"I'm not complaining. Stan's a good guy, but he's got his faults.
Women. So I play around too, just because . . ." She took a beat,
then suddenly her voice sagged. "I get so damn lonesome sometimes," she said slowly.

The real Maddy Phillips unexpectedly broke through. It was a
brief but revealing moment. Maddy had been almost successful in
her complete camouflage. Edith averted her eyes. She didn't want
Maddy to see her look of pity.

"I'm due at CBS," Edith said, quickly covering the embarrassed
pause. "They're showing that Madame Gres coat on the Sam Carter
show. I want to be sure *Tempo* gets name credit."

Maddy pulled the check away from Edith. "This one's on the expense account."

"Some racket," Edith said as they walked toward the door of the
restaurant.

"Don't make fun," Maddy said, signing the check. "One day I
may fall apart at the seams, and you may be fashion editor of
Tempo with a little expense account all your own."

They walked outside into the bright midday sunlight. "See you
later." Then with a clank of bracelets Maddy waved her off.

Edith hurried toward Madison Avenue and Fifty-second Street.
She paused at a plush dress salon and looked in the window at the
mannequin. Suddenly she caught the reflection in the glass pane of a
tall, attractive girl with soft red hair. She stared in fascination at the
image. Karen. Her lips formed the name silently. In another instant
reality dissipated the mirage. Edith was staring at her own reflection.

It seemed to be a turning point. For days after that everything
went wrong. Everything took on the flat monotone grayness of despair. It even showed in her work.

"I'm not asking any questions," Maddy said to her. "It's none of
my business, but if you don't snap out of it . . ." She paused and
looked at Edith kindly. "You're edging toward the breaking point. I
ought to know. I've been there myself a couple of times."

"I don't know what you mean," Edith replied, flustered.

"Just forget about the guy—and it must be a guy, *n'est ce pas?*" Maddy asked rhetorically.

"In a way."

"Then find another one," Maddy went on practically.

Edith couldn't help smiling. "What I'd really like to find is an apartment."

"How about Tom Eddy's?" Maddy said, referring to the art director. "He's moving from a three-room apartment on Sixty-third right off Lexington."

Maddy had another bright idea. She wanted *Tempo* to furnish the apartment and photograph its progress with Edith living there as a special monthly feature to entice career girls. The staff went to work with decorators. White vinyl covered the foyer. There was a red chenille rug in the living room, and a pink one in the bedroom. It was a warm setting for the provincial furniture. The apartment began to look as if it belonged in the pages of a magazine. But it was home for Edith, a panacea that almost obliterated the virulent past.

But it only took one phone call to bring back a flood of memories. The call was from Paul Levitt.

"Edith? This is Paul Levitt. Remember?"

Her hand holding the receiver began to tremble. She never thought she would hear that voice again. The years dropped away, leaving only the two of them and their brief, deliriously happy interlude.

"Paul Levitt," she said into the phone. Her voice was faint.

Time was turning back, after all. Back to ten years and a little flat on Lexington and Fiftieth Street. And Karen, and a tall, dark, serious young man with horn-rimmed glasses who was studying law.

"Paul Levitt," she said again into the phone.

"It's been a long time, Edith. Ten years," the pleasant, low masculine voice was saying at the other end of the line.

"Paul . . . how . . . how did you find me?"

Edith heard the low responding chuckle. She had almost forgotten how much she used to like to hear him laugh.

"*Tempo* magazine, naturally," he said. "Didn't you know you were a celebrity?"

"The apartment," Edith said. "Of course. The photographs in *Tempo*."

"I thought you were living in Paris."

"And I thought you were living in Utica," she answered.

"Not by a long shot. I'm just three blocks away from you right now. And that's three blocks too far, so how about lunch?"

"You mean today?"

"One o'clock at the Four Seasons, okay?"

"One o'clock," she said into the telephone.

She looked at her watch. One hour to go. One more hour and then . . . could they make up for ten lost years? Why not? It could start again perhaps just as fast as it ended. There was no Karen to keep her from Paul Levitt this time.

CHAPTER 17

The doorman at the Four Seasons swung the heavy glass doors open for her. She wondered whether he would still look the same. But even more she wondered whether she would look the same to him. She glanced into the antique mirror on the foyer wall and touched her soft red hair. It was too dark to see whether the years had left any noticeable mileage on her face. Then she felt someone touch her shoulder.

"Edith?"

She turned around. A warm, smiling face. Horn-rimmed glasses. Slightly graying hair. The scent of tweed and tobacco. It was all startlingly familiar. The years had been kind to him.

"Let's go upstairs," he said, taking her arm intimately. "I have a reservation."

"I didn't recognize you at first," Paul said after they sat down at a plush table beside an oblong pool that centered the luxuriant room.

"Have I changed that much?"

He looked at her as if he were trying to memorize her face. "It was the red hair that threw me off," he said finally. "You know something? It makes you look exactly like Karen." Then he said, "It's wonderful to see you again."

She tried to smile. She felt so ill at ease, as if they both belonged to another time and another place. But he appeared not to notice it.

"Well, I'm glad you finally decided to come home," Paul said. "I never thought Paris was a good idea in the first place. Remember?"

"How could I forget?" Edith replied.

"It's been so long . . ." he said, "I didn't even think you'd remember me at all."

"I've never stopped remembering," she said.

"Nor I. Why you and"—he paused momentarily—"and Karen were the best-looking girls in New York." He shook his head.

"Karen. It doesn't seem possible, does it? It was a terrible thing. She was a real beauty. So vibrant . . . so alive."

"Let's order," Edith said quickly as the captain walked over. Karen. Karen again. It was always Karen.

As soon as they gave the order Paul resumed the conversation that fascinated everyone who had known her.

He lowered his voice. "I was shocked when I read about it. Couldn't believe my eyes. I still can't. I keep asking myself . . . Why? Why did she do it? She had everything she ever wanted. Mike Hewlitt is a fabulously wealthy man. Have you ever met him?"

"Yes. Yes, we've met," Edith said.

"I can't figure it out. That's what I said to the police. It just didn't make sense."

"The police?" Edith looked at him startled.

"The one in charge of the case. Gerald. No, Gerard. That's it. Lieutenant Gerard."

"But why should you have gone to the police?"

"I didn't. They came to me."

"They came to you?"

"Of course. Standard procedure. An investigation before the inquest, naturally. And when they discovered I was her first husband —well, there you are."

Edith stared at him.

"I'm afraid I wasn't much help," Paul went on. "After all, we were only married for ten months, you know."

"No," Edith said numbly. That was all she could say. Just . . . no.

Paul looked at her sharply. "Of course you knew. You knew we were divorced. You must have known."

Edith kept staring at him. She was painfully conscious of his words. They were clear and concise. Simple statements of fact. Paul and Karen were married. Paul and Karen were divorced. Finally she spoke. "I don't believe it," she said softly.

"Edith." Paul took her hand. "She wrote you about our marriage. She told me. She told me she heard from you all the time. I even used to send my regards."

"I never knew . . . never. Karen never mentioned you."

He shook his head. "The break with you, Edie . . ." He paused, reflecting. "I guess I was lost. And she was there and . . . well." He let it trail off helplessly. "Can you understand?"

"There are so many things I can't understand," she said slowly. "I was hoping that maybe . . . maybe you'd follow me. But you didn't. Not even a letter or a phone call. Not even a word."

"I was young and foolish," he said. "I was shattered."

She said unhappily, "Let's forget it, Paul."

"But I often think about it. Even now," he said. "Some things hang around in your mind. You know how it is? Well, I did try to reach you again. I thought maybe you'd reconsider. But it was too late. You had already gone to Paris. Karen was very sweet on the phone. She asked me over." He paused. "Then we started seeing a lot of each other. She said she didn't know before how much I had meant to her. I believed her. She could be very convincing."

"So you married her."

"If you could call it that. She never wanted me. Not really. She wanted things I certainly couldn't give her. Then she started running around with other men. Finally, I just cleared out. Toward the end she met Mike Hewlitt, so she wanted a divorce just as much as I." Paul fingered the design on the tablecloth. "I still don't know why she married me. She wasn't impulsive, or emotional. Everything she said and did was carefully calculated. That's why the suicide didn't figure. She wasn't the type."

"Unless the years changed her completely."

"Changed?" Paul laughed shortly. "Changed?" he said again. "Why, she hadn't changed a bit. Not a day, not even a second of all those years showed on Karen. She was still completely gorgeous, exciting, and calculating. She was everything she always was."

"You . . . you saw her again?" Edith stared at him unbelievingly.

"Of course. This last year I used to see her all the time."

"You saw her?"

"Naturally, I was her attorney. I was handling the divorce for her. Hewlitt didn't want to let her go. But she was determined to make the break."

"Paul"—Edith leaned forward—"do you suppose that could be the reason?"

"Nonsense! You know Karen. Cool as the proverbial cucumber. We were just starting proceedings. Karen wanted a large settlement. But Mike wouldn't consider a divorce at all. I advised her to get the divorce without his consent and forget about the money. She said she'd let me know. And we left it at that. She wasn't the least bit upset about it. I don't know what she really wanted. But Karen was always a mystery to me," he said. "I still can't figure why she married me, can you?"

"Because I left for Paris and she needed a fast replacement. I guess you were it, Paul. Karen couldn't exist without an audience." Edith was using compassionate restraint. The proper noun should have been—scapegoat.

For a moment neither of them spoke.

Then Paul said, "Could . . . could we see each other again?"

She wondered why he sounded so tentative, almost afraid she might refuse.

"Why not?" she responded warmly.

"As a matter of fact, I did try to see you in Paris, but I couldn't find your address."

"You were in Paris?"

"Several times. One of our clients is a perfume house. I go every November and every time I'd walk along the Rue de la Paix, I'd stare at the faces of girls walking by, hoping maybe I'd see you."

"I'm glad you found me this time."

"Pure accident. It was really my wife. When Marge showed me that magazine . . . I thought I'd drop through the floor. Marge doesn't miss an issue of *Tempo*."

She turned her head away and fumbled with her bag so he wouldn't see the sudden flush on her cheeks. How ridiculous she had been to think even for a second that he was as alone as she was. "How . . . nice," she said hollowly.

But he wasn't even looking at her. He was going on about his family and talking about snapshots, and he had already taken them out of his wallet, and now he was carefully arranging the snapshots on the tablecloth.

"Good-looking kids, aren't they?" he said with pride. "Of course, you can't really see Marge in this one. It's just a blur."

She pulled her eyes over to look at the picture. She had to say something. "And that's your house?" she managed to mumble.

"Marge wouldn't have a house if they gave it away," he said smugly. "And she's the boss. The only house we're interested in is an apartment house. Why, when Marge saw those do-it-yourself bookcases in that living room—that's when she showed me the magazine. And there was Edith Weston." Paul looked at her. "I still can't believe it."

"Paul," Edith said, "why did you really call me?"

"What kind of a question is that?"

"I was just wondering. That's all," she said.

"Your picture, your name—I kept remembering that little walk-up on Lexington Avenue, you and me and Karen, and those awful Italian dinners. It all came back when I saw that magazine. And then I thought, it sure would be nice to see you again. So here we are," he said.

"Yes, here we are," Edith said flatly.

"What makes you ask? It's perfectly natural, isn't it? To want to see you again, I mean." He paused. "What made you come back from Paris, Edith?" he said all at once.

She drew in her breath. "And what makes you ask that?"

"Because of Karen?" He looked at her closely. "You hadn't seen her in ten years. Of course, her death would be upsetting to you, but you and Karen weren't exactly on the best of terms, I gather. You've come a long way from home, Edith."

"New York is my home," she said unevenly. "Not Paris. I had no intention of remaining there forever." Why was he checking up on her motives? Did he know anything more about Karen's death? "Then, of course, there was this opening at *Tempo,*" she said carefully.

"Well, I'm glad you're here, anyway. Whatever your reason . . . there's no reason why we shouldn't remain friends. I thought we could meet from time to time." Her hand was on the table and he covered it with his.

The role of *bon vivant* and man-about-town seemed quite incongruous with the Paul she used to know. But then, how well did she really know him?

"We can meet, can't we?" he was saying intimately.

She drew her hand away. "For auld lang syne?" she asked tightly.

"Why not?" he said.

"I can think of a lot of reasons."

"Name one," he said to her.

"You didn't tell your wife you knew me, did you?"

"Honey, you're turning this into an inquisition," Paul said blandly.

"You didn't tell her, though, did you?"

"Why should I make her unhappy for no reason at all? In my profession, as an attorney, I meet a dozen women a week. Marge is a very sensitive person. I saw no reason to mention you," he said defensively.

"I see."

"You don't see at all, do you?" he said, registering astonishment at the expression on her face.

"I don't see the point of going out with a married man," she said shortly.

He shook his head sadly. "You've got to get with it, honey. This is the twentieth century. We're not hurting anyone. Just because I happen to be married . . . well, that isn't exactly a jail sentence, you know."

"That's fairly obvious."

"Edith! You make one lunch date sound like a multitude of sins."

"Is that all you intended—one lunch date?"

"I told you," he replied. "I see no reason why we can't go on see-ing each other. You still mean a hell of a lot to me. I don't want you to disappear again."

She forced a smile. "I appreciate the sentiment, Paul. But, like Marge . . . I'm sensitive too."

He paid the check in silence. Neither of them spoke as they walked through the corridor adorned with costly murals, then down the carpeted stairway toward the front door.

He started to speak, then cleared his throat awkwardly. "If you don't want me to call you . . . okay," he said. "But you know where I can be reached. Just pick up the phone book and dial my number." They walked outside into the cold, gray day.

She nodded silently. Then she turned and left him standing there in the street, staring after her until she was out of sight.

CHAPTER 18

The board meeting was called for 10 A.M. Alan knew this was an important one because it was to be held in the big conference room next to J. C. Chanin's office.

The regular team was in the room . . . Tom Belding, the Carter account boy; Emerson Trask, head of the sales division; J.C.'s secretary, Mrs. Thompson; Dick Parnes, the account executive for Kingly Cigarettes; and Phil Oates, the art director of the agency. Something big was coming up. It was a meeting of the top echelon.

Alan started to whistle softly the refrain of "Hail, Hail, the Gang's All Here," when Mrs. Thompson stopped him with a sharp look. For all his sardonic appraisal of the setup, it was nevertheless reassuring that he was once again included in the inner sanctum. Just a month ago, he was in solitary confinement with the current issue of *Variety*.

At that moment, Chanin entered the conference room with Mike Hewlitt. Alan did a fast double take. But fortunately it was something he figured. He was ready. *Semper paratus*. J.C. had given him all the advance notice he needed. Hewlitt nodded briefly down the length of the table, then he and Chanin sat down. The show was on.

"First of all, gentlemen," said Chanin, "I'm happy to inform you that the Hewlitt account has been reinstated." A murmur of approval went around the table.

"As some of you may know, Mike was thinking of retiring, but as Mike certainly knows, we're delighted he changed his mind."

Hearty laughter followed. Alan was silently applauding Chanin's "sincere" technique.

"At any rate," Chanin continued, "I hope all of you, whom I consider my key men, will come up with some original hard-selling ideas for the new campaign. We're all here right now for the sole purpose of selling automobiles, so go ahead, boys." He waved his hand expansively. "Tee off."

Alan spoke first. "This is the way I see it, John. I think we ought to get a good glamorous anchor first. Something with enough emotional appeal to sell the technical facts."

"I go along with you there, Alan," Belding said. "So far we've used only a highly technical approach in a tight competitive field."

"Don't underestimate the technical necessities," Emerson Trask interrupted. "After all, we're selling a highly technical product—a machine."

"Of course you're one hundred per cent right, Emerson," agreed Alan. "But I think we'll hit the nail on the head when we promote glamour. What actually is the man behind the wheel buying? He's buying . . ." Alan paused momentarily for effect, then hit it hard. "He's buying—a way of life!"

"A way of life," Phil Oates repeated thoughtfully. "I like that. It's something the art department ought to be able to translate."

"Could you elaborate a bit on that, Alan?" J.C. said encouragingly.

Alan spoke with confidence. His foot was in the door again.

Mike leaned forward in his chair. "Way of life," he said. "It sounds a bit ephemeral to me. Too nebulous."

"Just a second, Mike." Chanin turned toward him. "Maybe Prescott here can make it more specific."

"As a matter of fact, John," Alan said quickly, "I've been tossing this idea around for months.

"By 'way of life' I mean exactly this. The motorist psychologically will buy a car that represents everything he wants to be. He's in the driver's seat telling the world he's a great guy. And he's telling his neighbor he's in the chips. The car he drives is his financial barometer."

"That sounds solid to me," Belding said with admiration.

Alan began to feel easier. Belding was on his team.

"If we can sell a Hewlitt car to those who want to step up their social status, then we've opened up a new market right there. In this area we've never explored the power of snob appeal." Alan lit a cigarette and inhaled deeply. It was a stall for time. "We live in a competitive society," he went on, "and since the women of America hold the purse strings, we've got to reach that specific competitive market."

"It's an angle," Hewlitt said, yielding slightly. "But how would you corner that specific, super market?"

"Direct our campaign to the woman behind the man. From Maine to California and back again . . . in little towns and hamlets across the U.S.A. . . . it's the women of America who are behind the power struggle for prestige. I think we ought to hook up a powerful national campaign with a top snob appeal magazine—*Vogue* or *Harper's Bazaar*."

Emerson nodded. "What the well-dressed woman will drive."

Phil Oates said, "How about *Tempo?* There's snob appeal for you. They already have society women modeling cars?"

"Let's stay with *Vogue*," Alan said emphatically. "Tremendous readership."

"*Tempo* is made to order for this one, Alan," Dick Parnes said. "Besides, they might be more inclined to give us plenty of free space in return. You know the fashion editor, don't you? . . . Maddy Phillips?"

"That's right, Prescott," Chanin enthused. "You could tie in with them easily."

"Sure, John," Alan was forced to concur. There was no way out of this one. "I guess I could swing it. It might work out if Maddy Phillips gave it her personal touch," he said reluctantly. And not Edith Weston, he was thinking uneasily. That would be a tie-in he hadn't counted on.

"We could even build it further by running a profile on you, sir." Belding turned to Mike. "An industrial tycoon . . . the new hero of the American woman."

"I wouldn't buy that," Hewlitt said flatly.

"Wait a second, Mike," Chanin broke in. "We could follow the same type of format that *Fortune* magazine uses. A profile on one of the nation's top executives."

"How about 'Mike Hewlitt—the Fabulous Face of the Decade'?" Dick Parnes offered.

"It's too presumptuous," Hewlitt said.

"I don't go along with you on that, Mike," Chanin disagreed. "That's a new angle and, placed in a magazine like *Tempo*, we couldn't miss."

Hewlitt shook his head. "You know how I feel about personal publicity, John."

"But we'd stick just to the superficial glamour, Mike. After all, that's what glamour is, isn't it?" Chanin persisted.

They all turned toward Hewlitt, who sat there pensively. Finally he said, "Well, give it a try. Set up a few trial layouts and send them to my office."

"Thank you, gentlemen." Chanin rose from his chair. He nodded approvingly around the table.

The conference was over.

Tom Belding slapped Alan heartily on the back as they walked toward the corridor. "It was par for the course this time. Nice going, boy!"

Alan mopped his brow. "Thanks, Tom." He tapped his forehead. "Clickety, clickety. An idea born every minute."

"The Fabulous Face of the Decade," Belding said. "Not bad."

"We could even set it to music," Alan said caustically.

"Say, how about that?" Belding pondered. "A new singing commercial."

"Sure. Sure thing, Tom." Alan hurried away. "See you later, old man." He sped down the steps to his office.

Yes, it was par for the course, but there were plenty of sand traps looming up ahead. The tie-in with *Tempo* . . . he really boxed himself into that one. It was like handing Edith Weston the Fabulous Face of the Decade on a silver platter. His own head would be on that platter if she ever told Hewlitt of his suspicions. Alan Prescott —boy wonder—would be out pounding the Madison Avenue pavements. He had to stop Edith somehow. Now it was imperative.

He walked into his office and Pat followed him.

"How'd it go, boss?"

"Fine, just great, sweetie. Will you get Edith Weston on the phone? It's *Tempo* magazine." He scribbled the number on a piece of paper.

"Okay, boss." She took the slip of paper from his hand.

"Incidentally, I'm not taking any other calls for the next ten minutes," he said.

"Right, Mr. Prescott." She gave him a provocative smile as she walked out.

He had made his comeback. The office grapevine had already sent out its telegraphic messages. The only trouble was that this fairhaired boy was getting too many gray hairs. First Hewlitt. Now Edith. Why was it so vitally important to her to find out how Karen died? What difference did it make?

Hell, he thought angrily. Karen's dead. It doesn't really make any difference now. It only mattered to me when I thought Mike

Hewlitt was needling me out of my job. No, that's not true. Sure, I'd like to know what happened. But I'm willing to sacrifice the answer for eighty thousand dollars a year.

There's only one thing left to do, he thought finally. Get Edith on my team, play on her sympathy, maybe play it straight and tell her the Hewlitt account is at stake. If I could get her really involved with me, that would stop her from talking. The phone on his desk was ringing. He lifted the receiver and heard Edith's voice.

"Edith," he said. "I want to apologize, explain about the other night."

"I'm the one who should apologize, Alan." She sounded embarrassed. "It was stupid of me to run out on you that way. I've been worrying about it all week."

"Then you will see me again?" he asked anxiously.

"Of course." She sounded warm and receptive. Maybe it would be easier than he thought.

"Would you see me tonight?" he asked her quickly.

"If you'll come for dinner. You haven't even seen my new apartment and I'll bet you didn't know I can cook."

"You obviously have a talent for everything," he said smoothly. "And where's the new apartment?"

She gave him the address.

CHAPTER 19

It was pure fiction. Right out of a slick magazine. The whole apartment. The black and white living room methodically accented with red. The carefully placed bric-a-brac. The do-it-yourself bookcase that was too artfully compounded to be constructed by an amateur. Even the books lined up looked as though they were bought by the yard. It was all made to be looked at. Not lived in.

Alan gazed around with satisfaction. This was going to be easier than he thought. The whole setup was perfect. The intimate dinner for two in the dining foyer. The atmosphere right on cue—soft lights and sweet music in the background. The meticulous white organdy apron around Edith's red dress, an artful blend to her hair. The conducted tour of the rest of the apartment later, even though the rest was only the very proper bedroom, done all in pink.

He didn't know why tonight seemed different than other nights. He didn't know why she seemed different. Before she had always been reserved, aloof, almost enough to thwart his interest—almost. But tonight—tonight was going to be different. He knew it the minute he stepped into the apartment. He couldn't figure out what she wanted from him this time.

He watched her later in the living room as she poured brandy into two snifters.

"You seem to enjoy playing house," he said as she handed him a glass.

"Is it becoming, Alan?" There was a seductive smile on her face. An intimate inflection in her voice.

He had to restrain himself, remind himself to take it easy. The switch she had made was just a little too sudden, a little too obvious. As if she were putting on an act—an obvious hard-sell promotion. He knew she figured him to play right into her hands. But that wasn't what was going to happen. Not tonight. Tonight she was going to play right into his hands. Edith Weston had him figured wrong.

"Is it, Alan?" she asked again.

"Is it what?"

"Becoming. Playing house, I mean." Again the seductive smile.

"It's becoming, all right," he said. "All very consistent with your latest *modus vivendi*. Everything is very appealing," he added dryly. "Including you. But just what did you have in mind—a proposal?"

She caught the sarcasm in his voice. She laughed awkwardly. "This is no time for small jokes," she said.

"What did you expect me to think . . . after this full-scale production?" he asked her.

"You're the end, really." She sat down on a chair. "You're rude and unappreciative," she told him, trying to be matter-of-fact.

"Very true," he agreed imperviously. "But at least—not naïve. Soft lights, sweet music, and a dinner cooked by her very own dainty white hands." He paused. "Why?"

"Why not? Can't you accept anything at face value?"

"I passed that stage when I was ten," he answered.

Her face clouded slightly. "Why must everything have an ulterior motive?" she said.

"Because it does. Especially with you. And I don't like to be used," he said slowly.

This time his arrow found the target. She reddened. "Did it ever occur to you that maybe I was . . . just apologizing to you?" she said defensively. "I was really sorry about the other night . . . walking out on you that way."

"Yes, that occurred to me. But so did a couple of other things."

"Like what, for instance?"

"Like, for instance, meeting Mike Hewlitt. And like getting a job. And now . . ." He paused.

"And now?"

"By process of elimination I decided this evening has exactly one purpose," he said smoothly. "The thing with Hewlitt was a fizzle. So you decided I might come in handy again with a new approach to Mike. You were out to my last three phone calls. But not today. And tonight I get the full treatment. Why?"

She was trying desperately to control herself. "It seems my cooking had a disastrous effect on you." Her eyes went flat. "Or maybe it is Mike Hewlitt. Maybe you figure it wasn't such a fizzle after all. And maybe you figure that's a bad thing. You are the account executive for Hewlitt cars. If Mike found out how well we knew each other, he might begin to get the idea you make a specialty of his women."

"That's the unkindest cut of all," Alan said, unperturbed. "But maybe you've got something there. I admire his taste. He's quite a connoisseur."

"You're very clever, Alan," she said coldly. "But not clever enough. Your ulterior motives live in a glass house. I can see them playing that same broken record over and over again. You're still trying to stop me from seeing him. You're afraid he'll find out you put me up to it. And that wouldn't look good at Chanin and Chanin Advertising, would it? Well, I've got news for you. Mike Hewlitt is the reason I asked you here tonight. You're right. But whether you help me or not—nothing is going to stop me from seeing Mike Hewlitt again. Nothing."

He waited until she was through talking. He waited and listened. Then he put his glass down carefully on the white marble coffee table and walked over to where she sat and stood there looking down at her.

"Have you finished?" he asked quietly.

She got up from the chair and went to the windows and stared out into the darkness with her back toward him. He followed her. She kept her face turned away, so that he could only see the red hair and the slim back and the white of her skin where the dress was cut low around the neck, and the tiny pearls around her throat that were the same color as her skin.

"We're two of a kind," he said in a low voice. "Even if you won't admit it. And we're attracted to each other. Even if you don't like the idea." He paused. "Sure, I've got ulterior motives too," he said with candor. "Mike Hewlitt is one of them. Now we've got the account sewed up at the agency. And I won't let anyone spoil it. Your assumption was correct. That's one of my reasons for being here now. There's a chance—maybe just a slim one—that your probing around into Karen's death might upset the applecart. I can't afford that chance. I've got to stop you whether it means browbeating you or seducing you. I would do anything in my power to stop you. If necessary, I would even consider marrying you."

He couldn't see the expression on her face, but he knew that her eyes went flat again, and that her face flushed with a tinge of pink the way it always did when she got angry. The slim white hand that held the curtains back tightened on the material.

"Then you're a fool," she said with quiet fury in her voice.

"Am I?" he asked. "It would be to our mutual advantage, wouldn't it? Look at the reality of the situation. Not the soft lights and sweet music. We're not teen-age kids. And it's not easy for anyone to be alone. Especially a woman."

"Do you think for even one minute I would consider marrying you?" Her voice came back at him in a low, mumbled staccato.

"I haven't asked you," he went on evenly. "But if you needed me enough . . . you'd consider it, all right. Feelings are always stronger than logic . . . even your feelings. I know you've got plenty of them lying around loose somewhere. You just have to pull them together. Maybe someday you will. Then you'll be ready to get married. At the moment, you're not. And when you do marry . . . it will be to someone who's necessary to your scheme of things. But I don't think marriage is the issue. Because right now . . ." His fingers moved lightly on the soft white skin where the pearls were resting. "That brings up the other reason I'm here tonight. Because right now . . . you and I . . . are the only thing that matters. Not words. Not talk. Not anyone else. Just you and I."

She remained motionless. This time she didn't move away. Then in a voice that was almost a whisper she said, "Is that what you told . . . Karen?"

"Why can't you allow yourself to feel anything? Why must you always go back into the past?" he said.

"Because . . . because that's where Karen is."

"Forget Karen. Give Edith Weston a chance to breathe, a chance to live, a chance to love. She has it coming, hasn't she? Besides," he added, "you happen to be a very desirable woman."

"You have a funny way of showing it," she said.

"Why? Because I want something real? You're trying to be someone else and it isn't very becoming. You're trying to live Karen's life and it doesn't quite come off," he said.

"That was your idea, remember?"

"I can see you're not going to let me forget it. But you've carried it too far already. Instead of burying Karen Hewlitt, you're burying Edith Weston," he said.

"What difference does it make to you what I do with my life?"

Slowly, his hands went to her shoulders and he pressed them firmly. Then he turned her body around so that she was facing him. Her eyes were soft and bright and clear, her lips full and soft and moist. She had the look of an innocent child and a seductive woman all at once. At that moment he thought he had never seen anyone more beautiful or more desirable.

"Can't you tell?" he asked her. "Can't you see it in my face, can't you hear it in my voice? Why do you think I let you use me for a fall guy?"

She avoided his eyes. "I . . . I just don't want to get involved, Alan. I'm sorry . . . but I don't. There are other things . . . other people that have to come first now. Afterwards . . . maybe afterwards it could be different."

"There is no afterwards," he said quietly. "There is only now and you and I."

"I don't want to get involved with you, Alan." It was almost a whisper, a half-spoken denial of her real feelings, words that belied the truth. She was afraid of him because she didn't trust him, not completely.

"Please, Alan, give me some time to sort this out."

"All right, Edith. But remember, tomorrows can't be counted on forever."

He left her by the window, smiling slightly at the knowledge that with a bit more persuasion, she would be his.

CHAPTER 20

The next day *Tempo* was humming. The rarefied atmosphere was charged with electricity. Edith knew something big was in the offing the moment she stepped into her glossy cubicle with a window that was a condensed version of Maddy's expansive office.

She knew even before she heard the clanking of Maddy's bracelets, which always precipitated her arrival. Maddy appeared in the doorway of Edith's office.

"Darling," she gushed. "We're made!" Maddy flopped into the leather chair that was crowded next to Edith's desk and beamed at her beatifically.

Edith kept typing rapidly with her eyes on the page in front of her. "What's up?" she asked.

"Drop everything," Maddy said with a flourish. "This is terrific!"

Edith finished typing the sentence and pulled the sheet from the typewriter. "Just let me shoot these captions to the art department." She swung out of the office and handed the page to a typist, then moved back to her desk. "Don't tell me, let me guess. I'm getting a raise."

"No, but you will if this goes through," Maddy said. "I just got a hot call from Chanin and Chanin."

"No kidding?" Edith reached for a cigarette.

"They want a fashion tie-in with one of their products."

"Carter vitamins?"

"Hewlitt cars. Thirty full-page color ads." Maddy emphasized each word with relish. "Manna from heaven. What the well-dressed woman wears behind the wheel of a Hewlitt."

Edith sat back in her chair. "Sounds like manna from Prescott. Alan Prescott."

Maddy laughed. "He's a pretty smooth operator."

"So I've heard," Edith said, drawing on the filtered tip.

"No," Maddy went on. "This call was straight from J. C. Chanin himself. Do you realize what this could mean in billings?"

"I've got a pretty good idea." Edith named a figure and Maddy, with a slight smile, nodded.

"Near enough. Even better."

Edith gazed at her freshly manicured nails. Maddy Phillips inadvertently had opened another door that led to Mike Hewlitt. It loomed in front of her . . . tempting, irresistible. But she resolutely put it out of sight, out of mind. After last night, Mike Hewlitt was totally eclipsed.

"Chanin wants to get the whole thing set up, rough proofs, copy, the works, before he submits it to the client," Maddy explained. "And I want you to take over on this, Edith."

Edith gripped the desk. This was the chance she had wanted. This was the excuse she could have used to see Mike Hewlitt again. But the feelings that Alan awakened in her last night closed the door on Mike Hewlitt for good. She couldn't do anything now that would endanger his position with Mike Hewlitt.

"Sure, Maddy," she said. "As long as you handle all the logistics. I'll stay with the paper work, okay?"

Something in the tone of Edith's voice made Maddy look at her curiously. "What's the pitch, Edie?"

Edith flushed. "Nothing. Except I'd prefer to remain in the background. I'm not very good at personal appearances. Conferences . . . agency meetings—they make me nervous."

"Since when do you scare so easy?"

Edith leaned forward, partially supporting herself with her arms on the desk. "Remind me to tell you a story someday."

"About whom?"

"Mike Hewlitt."

"You know him?" A light of astonishment flickered in Maddy's eyes. "Well," she said getting up, "so much the better. And now I have to head for the Chanin agency. But don't wait up for me. It could take hours."

"I'll wait," Edith assured her. "I'm just as anxious as you are."

"Good." Maddy crossed her fingers. "I may need someone to pick up the pieces."

"You mean, you want me to be your cheering section? I'm your girl!"

Maddy looked at her watch. "Hang on to those cheers, kid.

Sometimes the best-laid plans oft go astray." Then she made a hurried exit.

It was shortly after six o'clock when Maddy came back to her office. Most of the staff had already gone home.

"How'd it go?" Edith asked her.

"Follow me and I'll show you," Maddy said. She flung herself onto the plump upholstered sofa at the far end of her office and squinted her eyes at the desk heaped with folders. "That," she indicated with a nod of her head, "is it."

Edith walked over to the desk and thumbed through the folders. "Cheers . . . and more cheers! You've got everything here except the automobile itself," Edith said enthusiastically.

Maddy sighed. "It was a long grind." She kicked off her shoes.

"What happened and who was there?" Edith asked eagerly.

"Chanin. He doesn't talk much. Alan Prescott. He had plenty to say."

"Well, Alan was on our team. He must have been in there pitching all the way!"

"But he wasn't," Maddy said. "That's the funny part and that's why it took so long. He kept throwing monkey wrenches into everything that I proposed. I can't understand that guy. I sort of counted on him for smooth sailing. And he does carry a lot of weight. After all, he is the account executive."

"You didn't happen to mention me, did you?"

"Sure. I told him right off you would work on this along with me."

Edith sat down on the edge of Maddy's desk and shook her head slowly.

"What's the matter?" Maddy asked.

"If I'd only had time to think, I would have told you to forget about me as far as the Hewlitt account is concerned." Edith pressed her hand to her forehead. "I really goofed."

"I don't know what you're talking about," Maddy said, puzzled. "But forget it, Edith. I barely had time to get there. Who had a chance to think?"

"What about Hewlitt?" Edith tossed off the question casually. "Was he there?"

"He couldn't make it," Maddy said. "But we, I mean you, have an appointment with him in a few days. We'll get something tangible worked out."

"But, Maddy, I—"

"Unless friend Alan persuades Chanin otherwise. And I have a hunch he's going to try," Maddy said. "I didn't tell Alan I was going to send you over to Hewlitt. That's going to be a last-minute switch."

Edith paced the office restlessly.

"Please. Sit down." Maddy groaned. "You're making me nervous."

"Look, Maddy." Edith sat down in the chair again. "Forget about me. You take over, you follow through on this. You see Hewlitt."

"Great," Maddy said with a complete lack of enthusiasm. "The only trouble is, I can't do it. I have to be in Paris."

"Paris! Why Paris?"

"That's the whole pitch," Maddy said. "You know that new designer—Pierre Rousse?"

Edith nodded. "Used to sketch for Dior, didn't he?"

"That's the one," Maddy replied. "Now he has his own house. He's going to design a whole new line exclusively for the Hewlitt series in *Tempo*. The well-dressed woman behind the wheel of a Hewlitt."

Edith whistled. "Wow. That's quite a tie-in."

Maddy grinned and cupped her ear with her hand. "You can make with more cheers now."

"You mean it was your idea?"

"All mine," Maddy said. "Chanin put the call through right then and there to Paris. They even made my plane reservations."

"I'm sure the whole campaign can be sewed up without me," Edith persisted.

"Be my guest," Maddy said. "You'll have to. No one else can do the job as well as you."

"You can. A whole lot better," Edith said. "Let me go to Paris instead. I know my way around there in the dark."

"Sure you do," Maddy agreed. "In fact, that's the pitch Alan made. He wants you to go to Paris. He wouldn't let up."

Edith looked at her quickly. "Alan?" Why should Alan want her to go to Paris? After last night . . .

"He kept insisting that you're the one to see Pierre Rousse. He wants me to stay in New York and meet Mike Hewlitt," Maddy said.

"So he wants me to go," Edith said slowly. She saw him now sitting in her apartment, and she remembered his words. "I would do anything in my power to stop you," he told her. He told her before the fact and she let him get away with it. He warned her in advance, and she was stupid enough not to realize what he was doing. Stupid enough, seduced enough, to turn her back on the chance she was waiting for. Leave it to Alan. He would do anything for a job. Nothing else mattered to him. She could go to China as far as he was concerned. She meant nothing to him. He just wanted her as far away as possible. Was he afraid she would get too close to the truth or was it just his job?

"Alan's a slick operator," Maddy was saying. "He almost had me convinced."

"And me," Edith murmured.

"What?"

"Nothing," Edith said. "I was just agreeing with you."

"Anyway," Maddy went on, "he couldn't sell me the idea with all his fast talk. Because, well . . ." Maddy hesitated.

Edith looked at her curiously.

"Well . . ." Maddy paused. "This isn't for publication. But I thought I might take a hop over to London while I was there. Just for a few days," she added uneasily.

Edith sensed Maddy's distress. "London?" she asked. "What's London got that New York hasn't?"

"Stan," Maddy said.

For a moment the name meant nothing. Then Edith suddenly remembered. Stan. Maddy's husband. Of course.

"Sorry. For the moment I forgot," Edith said.

"I almost forgot myself," Maddy said. There was an odd expression in her eyes. "It's been more than six months."

Edith said, "He must be anxious to see you."

"I wonder," Maddy said tonelessly.

"I keep writing but . . ." She broke off suddenly. "Never mind about me. I talk too much," she said briskly. "We've got more important things to settle."

"It's already settled, Maddy," Edith said with finality. "I'll handle the Hewlitt account. There's nothing I'd like better."

"Good." Maddy looked relieved. "And you say you've already met Mike Hewlitt?"

"Yes, we've met."

"I'd feel awfully guilty about going, Edith, if you were going to be involved in something unpleasant."

"Maddy, stop worrying."

"The whole responsibility will be on your shoulders. I hate to do this to you, Edith, but it's all organized for you anyway," Maddy said. "All on paper right in front of you. There's another angle. Mike Hewlitt—Fabulous Face of the Decade. You have to interview him for a profile series."

Maddy went to her desk and pulled out a typewritten page from the stack of papers. "Here it is," she said.

Edith read the page over quickly. "How many installments?"

"It should run for three. That's what we promised to deliver. You see, the whole concept is to sell Mike Hewlitt to our public. The fashion-conscious woman. There's just one thing you have to remember at all times," Maddy told her.

"What?"

"Don't dig too deep. This isn't supposed to be an exposé. We just want the . . ." She paused, groping for the right word. "The Pablum," Maddy said. "That's all. Nothing personal."

"I understand."

"That was the only way he would buy the idea in the first place. If you look over that paper you'll see the kind of lead questions we've jotted down." She picked up a pencil. "His wife died some time ago," she said as she made notations on the page.

Edith remained silent.

"But don't mention that. You can talk about his town house. Describe the interior, if he'll let you get a look at it. Describe his office, his business, his face, his personality—but keep away from his personal life." Maddy paused and looked at her curiously. "How did you meet Mike Hewlitt?"

Edith shrugged her shoulders before she answered. "Oh, we just met once at a cocktail party," she said easily. "You know. Over a drink. That was all."

"Oh," Maddy said. "Well, even that's something to go on." She put the pencil down on the desk. "That's all there is. The rest is up to you. If you run into serious trouble," she added, "just call me in Paris. I'll leave you the number where I can be reached. Two more days and then Paris—the George V Hotel.

"And maybe I still have time to soften up Alan before he hears I'm the one who's going, not you."

"Alan?"

Maddy nodded. "I know he's going to put the pressure on. He asked me for dinner tomorrow night to talk things over. That's all right with you, isn't it?"

"Why shouldn't it be?"

"Oh, I dunno," Maddy said vaguely. "I thought perhaps you . . . well, maybe you and Alan were . . ." She stopped abruptly. "I guess I should stop speculating. I don't know what gave me the idea."

"It's rather obvious. Alan and I are as far apart as the poles," Edith said coldly.

Maddy smiled. "That's what gave me the idea."

"Well, you're wrong."

"Of course," Maddy said. "Anyway, I just wanted you to know our dinner date tomorrow night is pressure, not pleasure."

CHAPTER 21

Maddy Phillips dressed for dinner meticulously. She pulled on a black wool sheath, and massed strands of turquoise at her neck. She critically appraised her reflection in the full-length mirror, then sat down wearily at the *poudre* in her dressing room. The mask-like makeup was no longer capable of achieving the complete coverage she depended on. Fool the public, she thought grimly to herself. It wasn't going to work much longer.

Maddy's tapered heels clicked across the floor as she moved from the dressing room through the large comfortable bedroom into the living room. It was a five-room apartment on Eighty-first Street and Park Avenue. On clear days from the windows facing east you could even see the East River.

She remembered when she and Stan found the apartment. It was five years ago, the day after they were married. Maddy was nearly forty, but when she met Stan she knew that's why she had waited so long. This was it. Three months later she knew this would never be it. There was another woman. But she kept hoping he would get over it. Oh, he got over it, all right. Except there was another woman after that. And then finally she stopped counting because she knew there would always be another woman.

So she found other men. One was Alan Prescott. It was at a cocktail party. Stan was in Europe. She was lonesome and had too many drinks. And, well, Alan was there. Available. After a while the liquor and the men seemed to be more necessary and more available.

The marriage went on as if there was a tacit agreement between them not to admit failure. If they were divorced she would have nothing, be nothing. An admission of defeat was out of the question. She would be losing Stan, losing face. This way was better than no way. This way she could at least pretend. What was a woman without her dreams? Take those away and only half a woman is left.

Maddy resolutely picked up the phone resting on the antique rosewood desk. For the third time in a week she placed a transatlantic call to Stan in London. The operator said she would try the number again and call her back. Even as Maddy hung up the phone she had the feeling that it was useless. Just like before.

But maybe this time, she thought. Maybe this time. The operator rang back.

"Mrs. Phillips?" the operator said.

"Yes?" Maddy caught her breath. If she could only hear Stan's voice again everything would be all right.

"Mrs. Phillips," the operator was saying, "on your call to London . . . that party does not answer. Would you like me to try again in ten minutes?"

Maddy's hand tightened on the receiver until the knuckles became white.

"Never mind, operator."

"I can try again later this evening," the operator said.

"No. Just cancel the call, please. Thank you."

Maddy slowly hung up the phone. She could call him again, after she arrived in Paris. Of course Stan would be out now, she thought. How could he possibly know she was going to phone him from New York? She was being foolish. Did she expect him to hang around an empty one-room flat waiting for a phone call he didn't even know about?

She walked over to the liquor cabinet and took out a bottle of scotch. Just a short one, she promised herself. She poured out one jigger and downed it rapidly. Then another. That was better. Now just one more. That ought to do it. Three drinks. A warm glow, a blurring of the senses, an uplifted feeling of euphoria. God, how she needed these drinks. One used to do the trick. But not anymore. She poured out another one and drank it in one gulp.

She was beginning to feel better already. She replaced the bottle in the cabinet and started to hum a tune as the doorbell rang. She glanced at the clock over the mantel. Alan was exactly on time.

Maddy moved toward the door. She gave her black hair a last-minute pat, then carefully arranged her features in a vivid smile, as she opened the door.

It wasn't until they finished dinner at Ratazzi's that Alan finally steered the conversation around to automobiles and Edith Weston.

Alan finished his coffee, then he said, smiling, "Now I feel fortified. How about you?"

Maddy nodded, sipping crème de menthe. "Fire away, sweetie. After that dinner nothing could faze me."

"Maddy," Alan said seriously, "you know how much I respect your ability as an editor."

"That's a good enough opening," Maddy said with a short laugh. "Always disarm the opponent first with a fast compliment."

"Since when are we opponents?" Alan said. "I thought we were on the same team."

"So did I," Maddy said. "Until that conclave in Chanin's office."

"Everyone at the agency feels the same way about you. That's why we wanted space in *Tempo*. You're first choice."

"But?" Maddy inquired.

"But," Alan repeated, "we want to pick *your* brains—nobody else's."

"I can't do the whole job alone, Alan. Edith's very capable. You recommended her yourself," Maddy reminded him.

"Of course she's capable, Maddy," Alan said impatiently. "But we're committing ourselves for over three hundred thousand dollars in space. And we want the best editor in New York right on the job from start to finish."

"Very flattering," Maddy said sweetly. "I thought you were selling cars—not soft soap."

"Maybe I can do both," he replied.

"I'll bet you can," Maddy concurred.

Alan lit a cigarette and handed it to her, then lit one for himself. "And there's one other thing, Maddy," he said. "In addition to the space we're buying, we want the profile series . . . the Fabulous Face of the Decade."

"In the way of *free* space, you mean," Maddy said.

"You got the message." Alan smiled. "Clothes and cars make the woman. Fashion is divine and all that, but so is money. So what do you say? That's a big hunk of space we're prepared to buy. But we want a big hunk of free editorial space in return. Fair exchange?"

"Do we have any choice?" Maddy asked dryly.

"Not a bit," Alan replied smoothly. "We'll talk mink, if you talk turkey."

Maddy shrugged her shoulders. "You win, Alan. You know darn well I'm not going to lose out on that account."

"But we want you with it all the way," Alan reminded her. "No assistants taking over."

Maddy looked at him phlegmatically and shrugged her shoulders.

Alan walked back to his apartment after taking Maddy home. He wasn't satisfied with the evening. He had the feeling somewhere along the line that Maddy wasn't with him at all. But there was nothing else he could do. Because what Maddy didn't know, was that John Chanin had already okayed *Tempo* magazine. Mobile fashions and Hewlitt cars were going full speed ahead in *Tempo* whether Maddy or Edith was behind the wheel. The evening was one of purest waste.

CHAPTER 22

Kennedy Airport. Maddy waving as she boarded the plane. Edith watching the gigantic silver Pan American bird circle the field, then finally take off into the horizon. Paris. That was yesterday. Today Maddy would be in Paris. Today Edith wished that she could have gone instead.

She watched the hands of the clock in her office slowly edge around, bringing her closer and closer to the ominous hour. Then she got up from her desk, picked up a manila envelope, put on her coat, and left the office.

It was a glass-brick edifice at Forty-sixth and Park Avenue. She entered the shining lobby adorned with cubist murals and indirect lighting, and made her way into one of the jammed express elevators which rose silently and rapidly upward. She had the feeling that she was in a soaring plane, vacuumed in outer space, and for a moment she was caught in the panic that embraced her when she was planing from Paris to New York three months ago. The flight into the unknown. The terrifying flight from fantasy into reality.

"Tower floor," the elevator operator was saying, and Edith found herself alone in a huge softly lit corridor paved with thick white carpeting. She walked resolutely toward the double glass doors which bore the legend HEWLITT ENTERPRISES printed in gold letters. A dignified receptionist looked up as she entered.

"Your name, please," the receptionist asked her, with a pencil poised over a memo pad.

"Edith Weston," Edith replied. "I have an appointment with Mr. Hewlitt at two o'clock."

She sat down on the modern banquette along the wall, opposite three men who were carrying tan leather portfolios. Her manila envelope seemed quite out of place. Shabby by contrast.

She felt as if she were approaching an operation. At any moment, she expected to see the men in white, attended by uniformed nurses, push a stretcher through the receptionist's area. They would come toward her. Someone would ask her to check her valuables at the desk. Someone would approach her with a long white sheet of paper filled with questions. Her name. Her age. Her place of birth. Did she have any childhood diseases? Where did she live? What did she do? The name of her closest of kin? Karen Hewlitt. Deceased. May 10th. This year. Died of poisoning. Suicide. Or was it . . . murder?

"Miss Weston to see Mr. Hewlitt," the receptionist whispered into the intercom box on her desk, then clicked the button.

Another lapse of time. Then a gray-haired woman walked into the outer office.

"Miss Weston?" She inclined her head slightly toward Edith.

"Yes?" Edith looked up at the austere woman regarding her intently.

"This way, please."

Edith rose and followed the woman into a long corridor.

They walked along wordlessly, one after the other, the only sound in the corridor the sound of their footsteps.

Finally the woman paused in front of a large oak door at the farthest end of the hallway. She tapped lightly on it, then turned the knob.

"You may go in, Miss Weston," she said, and left Edith standing on the threshold of Mike Hewlitt's office, alone and unarmed except for the brown manila envelope which she clutched firmly in her hand. She drew in a breath.

"Well, Edith."

The blue piercing eyes stared at her from the other side of a desk. He was wearing a dark gray suit and the somber intense expression she remembered so well. He was like a bulwark of disenchanted, ominous strength.

"How are you, Mike?"

"Very well," he said.

She had forgotten the impact of his low, resonant voice. She slowly came toward the desk and sat down on the edge of a white leather chair placed at a relatively closer position to the desk. She looked around the extraordinary room. There were no windows that were visible. The room was vast, soundproofed. The sudden thought struck Edith that there were no identifying marks of personality to be seen anywhere. It could have been a magnificent president's office in the window of Sloane's. It was a disembodied inner sanctum of prestige, power, and wealth. Beyond that it revealed nothing. It was a room of complete concealment. Edith moved uneasily in her chair.

"I was quite surprised when my secretary told me to expect you," he said. "I thought you'd be in Paris by now."

"Miss Phillips is covering the Pierre Rousse showing in Paris," she faltered.

"I didn't mean that. I meant your sudden change of plans. Last time you said you were . . . just a tourist."

"Oh, that." She knew her smile was too artificial, her voice too bright. "I'm a real New Yorker now. Your personally conducted tour of Manhattan was irresistible," she went on. "You see how convincing it was."

"Odd how we keep running into each other, isn't it?" His fingers made a tapping sound on the desk. "Of course, you could call it coincidence." There was a slight knowing smile on his face. "The long arm of coincidence. It's really working overtime. How did you get this job at *Tempo* anyway?"

"An old friend of mine," she answered nervously. "Alan Prescott. I looked him up again when I got to New York."

"You really get around, don't you?" There was a curious edge to his voice.

"Not really."

The words, the answers, came automatically. The impact of his presence on her was even stronger than before. All she could think of was that she had never expected to see him again. And now she could reach out and touch him if she dared. His closeness overwhelmed her. She wanted to know why he hadn't called her, but again she dared not ask. He terrified her and he fascinated her. It was just like the other times.

"So now you're here to stay," he said. She could have cried at the impersonal tone of his voice. It's no use, she thought. No use at all. He wasn't even showing a flicker of interest.

"If you want . . . I can ask for a reassignment," she said in desperation. "I'm hardly indispensable at *Tempo*."

For a moment he didn't reply, his fingers tapping the desk again. "Never mind. Let's move on to the Fabulous Face of the Decade." He said it with just a shade of sarcasm, just enough to annoy her.

She fumbled with the papers in the folder, wondering how she could get through to him, break down this meaningless, cold façade. She sat very still and looked at him. Suddenly . . . she said, "Mike, why didn't you phone me?" She was appalled at the sound of her own words—they slipped out, unexpected. It was an uncontrolled, inadvertent question. She was embarrassed. But the directness hit the target.

Mike reacted. She could see it in his face. He answered carefully. "Your resemblance to my wife is very disturbing to me. Any other questions?" he asked tightly.

"I'm sorry," Edith faltered. "I didn't mean to . . . to be rude. It's just that . . . that . . ." She paused. "It doesn't matter," she said finally.

"Go on. It's just what?"

"The things you said to me," she plunged ahead again. The words stumbled out. It was too late to retreat. "There seemed to be something more between us than just a casual meeting. I wanted to see you again. You're the reason I decided to stay on in New York. It's only because of you. I mean . . ." She stopped suddenly. She felt her face flush, redden.

He sat there silently, studying her carefully. Then he replied coldly, "Obviously it *was* more than just a casual meeting. Now shall we skip the personal interview and get on with the one that's for public consumption?"

It was the final humiliation. Her face was crimson. She tried to control the tears that were about to spring into her eyes. She succeeded in making a complete fool of herself. She hadn't thought for a second it would be easy, but she hadn't counted on playing the idiot. She took a pencil and notebook from her bag and managed to get on to the questions that were prepared for the interview.

They talked about cars. Designs. Fashions. They talked about the Fabulous Face of the Decade. They talked about everything except Mike Hewlitt, the man. He was being very cooperative now. Polite. Courteous. Solicitous. Then finally it was over. She got up to leave.

"I'm supposed to take a few photographs of your home," she said tentatively.

"My home? Why my home?"

"It's just an idea that *Tempo* had," she fumbled, "to sell you to the women of America."

"I see. Well, that can be arranged. I'm usually home in the evenings." He was even friendly. In fact, very friendly.

She was confused—the way he always managed to confuse her. Were her fears baseless, even a little absurd? Was he really the monstrous person that had dwelled in her imagination, whose ominous form was so insistently sustained by Alan? She could not quite reconcile the image of the dire villain with this mercurial hero of the decade. Yet she couldn't completely jettison the warnings of Alan. Once again she felt the faint and familiar throb of doubt. She was anxious to leave.

She quickly gathered up the papers and moved toward the door.

"I'll have my secretary phone you. Let her know which evening will be most convenient for you to be at my home," he said cordially.

She paused at the door. "Could I bring a cameraman along?"

Mike looked at her and she detected a hint of amusement in his eyes.

"Apparently," he said, "there's one woman of America who doesn't want to be sold."

Edith laughed nervously. "I just thought I might save you some time."

"I told you," he said, "I'm rarely busy in the evenings. Besides, I happen to be a fairly good cameraman myself. Photography is a favorite hobby of mine. So I think it would save even more time if you came alone."

Edith flushed and stood at the door silently.

He looked at her curiously. Then he said, "It might be a good idea if you scanned the house first by yourself. Then you would know exactly what you wanted to have photographed."

"Yes. You're right, of course," Edith said quickly. "Your secretary will phone me?"

"Miss McAvity will be in touch with you in a day or so," Mike said. He nodded to her pleasantly as the phone on his desk rang. Edith left as he picked up the receiver.

As she walked rapidly down the corridor, nodding on the way out to Miss McAvity, the faint pang of doubt suddenly became more acute. She wondered why he insisted upon seeing her alone.

CHAPTER 23

It was a sharp cloudless night. The kind of a night that exposed all the stars in the sky. As Edith walked up Park Avenue she knew it was going to be a night to remember. Mike Hewlitt was home. He was waiting for her.

Inadvertently, Edith's pace became slower. She looked at her watch. Five of eight. She was due at eight-fifteen. She breathed in the crisp autumn air and her arm tightened around the small manila folder. Cars and people passed her by. She felt alone and anonymous, caught up in the stream of perpetual motion that was New York.

She glanced up at the street sign. Sixty-fourth Street. Four more blocks and she would at last step over the threshold where she could meet the past, face to face.

She approached Sixty-eighth Street and turned west toward Madison, then on to Fifth Avenue. Number 5. Just across the street. She stepped down from the curb. A low-slung black car sped around the corner and suddenly it swerved toward her. She heard someone scream. Her heart quickened and she stopped. Gerard's warning flashed through her mind. A man pulled her arm and she was yanked back on the sidewalk. She stumbled against the curb. Her pocketbook fell to the ground. The car sped by.

"Are you all right, lady?"

A strange man helped her back on the sidewalk. A few people stood around her in a little circle staring.

"That was a close call," someone else said. "That character nearly ran you over!"

Edith drew in her breath and started to tremble. A woman held out her pocketbook.

"Thank you," she said, shaking.

"Missed you by a fraction of an inch," the man said. "It's a good thing I was standing near you."

"Thank you very much." Edith drew in her breath. "I didn't even see it coming." She started to move away, embarrassed by the curious onlookers. The small group started to disperse.

"The car looked like a Hewlitt Eighty," the man said. "But it was going so fast I couldn't see the driver. It must have been a woman. Some dames drive crazy." He shook his head. "Next time watch your step," he cautioned. "A bunch of lunatics driving these days." He started to walk off.

She tried to tell herself that it was accidental. It could have happened to anyone. A lot of people drive Hewlitt cars. She ought to know. But she was still trembling when she crossed the street. She stared into the dark emptiness. Who was driving that car? Mike Hewlitt . . . Paul . . . Alan? Three who knew Karen. Three who were close enough to Karen to love her—or hate her. Was one of these a murderer? Would she find the answer tonight here in this house? Was one of them watching her now—silently lurking in the shadows? Was one of them driving that car . . . afraid enough of the truth to murder her too? She shuddered and drew her coat closer. She was just having a bad case of nerves, she told herself. It could have happened to anyone crossing a street. She forced her eyes back to the mansion that loomed before her.

It was surrounded by a black wrought iron fence that stretched around to Fifth Avenue, banked by massive trees whose branches hung down over the railing almost touching the street below. She moved closer. Even in the darkness she could see the leaves bleeding with the colors of autumn foliage. A few streams of light peered out from heavily curtained windows. It was a mansion formed of white stone and marble. A formidable, secret mansion set far back from the steet. An island apart from the din and hubbub that circled it. A mansion that was obviously incommunicado. It might have been designed for death instead of designed for living.

Slowly, she walked up to the entrance that faced the side street. The iron gate was open. Again she wondered why Mike Hewlitt had refused to admit the staff photographer. She was afraid to enter this house alone.

She drew in her breath, clutched her envelope tighter, then walked unsteadily up to the front doors. She pressed a white button, and heard the soft tones of chimes ringing within. The brown oak doors were adorned with carved figurines. She could see at a glance that they were antique English panels, at least a century old. The doors opened. A butler in a black uniform nodded obsequiously.

"Miss Weston?" He barely waited for her affirmative reply. "You're expected. Come in, please."

She walked inside. The doors closed behind her. The entrance hall where she was standing could only be described as spectacular. It was white marble. All white marble. The floor. The walls. The ceiling. A long circular staircase curved its way from the floor to a ceiling high above. In the center of the vestibule a massive crystal and bronze chandelier hung low, its prisms twinkling and shining with rainbow hues.

"Would you step this way, please." The butler took her coat.

She followed him around the circular staircase to a double door that was closed. The butler knocked gently. She heard a man's voice respond from inside the room, and the doors opened. The butler quietly walked away. She stepped on deep-pile beige carpeting that cushioned her footsteps.

Mike Hewlitt came over to greet her. He wore a maroon smoking jacket, and a polite smile on his face.

"Good evening," he said.

She walked into the center of the room, then stared in wonder at the magnificence of the library. Brown and beige. Walls of books. Fabulous antiques. Luxurious fabrics—satins, velvets, damasks. She placed her folder carefully down on a highly polished fruitwood desk. She could feel him watching her, watching every move she made.

"It's rather large," he said quietly, in his low, deep voice. "You have to get used to it."

She turned to him. "I don't think I ever could," she said. She felt so cold, so chilled. Her hands were like ice.

"Well, this will do for a starter," he said as the butler entered holding a tray with two brandy snifters. She sat down in a chair and took one of the glasses.

He came to her and touched his glass to hers. "To a successful campaign, Edith," he said smoothly.

"Thank you." She sipped the golden liquid. She could feel its warmness going through her body, steadying her frayed nerves.

He went over to one of the paneled walls and pressed a button. Suddenly the room was filled with music.

"Tchaikovsky . . . the *Romeo and Juliet Overture*," he said.

Tonight he had changed over from the impersonal and inaccessible to the personal and accessible, as easily as he pressed buttons. It had its usual unsettling effect upon her. She gripped the glass tighter, then looked about the room.

It was the zenith of luxury. The exquisite antique furniture melted into the setting, giving it a monochrome effect of rich softness. The brown and beige coloring diluted into a blend of molten gold. The entire room, the high ceiling, the spaciousness . . . had an effect of oneness that made it seem even more enormous and more impersonal.

"What are you thinking?" he asked her.

"Just that this is the perfect background for the Fabulous Face of the Decade," she said. "It's magnificent."

He smiled. "I think you're beginning to create your own copy," he said.

"Not at all," she answered. "It's merely a tribute to your good taste."

"Would you like to see the rest of it?"

"I certainly would."

"Just follow me," he said, rising.

"What has to be censured shall not be recorded," he added lightly. "But then, of course, I really have no skeletons in my closets."

She looked at him sharply, but he was already leading the way from the study to the foyer. She followed him up the long circular staircase into room after room. There were bedrooms and guest rooms, and on the second landing, a magnificent dining room.

Then he paused in the corridor before a door that was closed, and he took a key from his pocket.

"This room," he said slowly, "hasn't been used in a long time. But I would especially like you to see it."

His face was inscrutable as he leaned over and unlocked the door. They stepped inside and he turned on the switch.

She drew in her breath. "It's a dream," she whispered. "I can't believe it's real." It was a delicate ivory boudoir adorned with Baccarat crystal. A scent of musky perfume, a soft yet heady fragrance, hung in the air. Her pulse quickened. That fragrance . . . it was so familiar, so familiar, even after all these years.

"It is a dream," he said cryptically.

She stared about her, at the ivory satin curtains, the white velvet chairs, the fragile writing desk. Then her eyes caught the opened book on the night table, the pages held apart by reading glasses. She gasped and closed her eyes tightly. She could see Karen sitting at the desk. She could see Karen lying on the bed. The pillow dented where her head was resting. The perfume seemed to be closing in on her now, stifling her. She was beginning to feel sick, dizzy.

She felt his hand touch her arm, then slide around her waist. He pulled her to him, closer, closer. His hands moved over her body. His mouth found her mouth and he started to kiss her hungrily, passionately. She felt weak, faint. She couldn't move. She couldn't speak. She could only stand there and let him make love to her. She was helpless with fear. Then suddenly—paralyzed by desire.

She wanted him to make love to her. She wanted to belong to him. She wanted him to possess her just as he had possessed Karen. She wanted this room to be hers, that bed to be hers, that book marked at the place where she had stopped reading. She wanted to belong to Mike Hewlitt.

She felt his warm mouth upon her neck, and his hands touching her face, and now he was leading her toward the bed. The fragile white bed that was still creased by the outline of Karen's body. She moved as in a trance. This was not real. This was a dream. And she was Karen. Edith Weston no longer existed. Somewhere in the dream she heard the faint tones of a clock chiming the hour. Karen's clock.

"No . . . no," she whispered. It was almost a moan. She pulled away from him. This was Karen's room. Her bed. Her husband. She must run from this room. Run from this man. She pulled herself away from him and ran toward the door, and stood there leaning on the wall. She must compose herself. She had to compose herself. She had to leave this room.

"Edith," he said. He followed her to the door, he held her arm.

"Please," she said in a low, trembling voice. "This room . . . it's so warm, so close. Please . . ."

"Of course," he said quickly. He switched off the light, and closed the door, locking it again. With his arm still around her he led her down the staircase in silence, back into the library.

Neither of them spoke. She picked up her brandy glass again and finished it. Then she looked at him. "Why . . . why," she asked in a low voice, "why did you want me to see that room?"

"Why?" he said, his voice tight with emotion. "I'll show you why."

Mike went to the fireplace and touched a panel. A spotlight went on and the whole wall above the fireplace became diffused with light. She stepped back and stared at the portrait that hung there. It was a portrait in oil. A painting of an exquisite woman.

"Karen!" Edith gasped the name in a voice she could barely recognize as her own. Alan had forewarned her. She knew about the painting. Even Mike had described it to her. But the shock of seeing it was too great. The portrait was almost human.

"Yes," Mike said. "Karen."

She stared at the portrait, her eyes focused on the image before her as if some force was holding her there. An aura of flame hair framed the porcelain face. The soft white skin looked alive, alive enough to touch. Edith could feel the impenetrable green eyes staring at her, mocking her. An involuntary shudder went through her body. So this was Karen ten years later. The lovely, breathtaking face was the same. The same as she remembered. The beautiful body was the same. Rounded, firm, encased in the voluptuous folds of a gleaming yellow satin gown. It was Karen. But a different Karen. What was different? Something about the face. The expression. The expression in the eyes was cruel, belying the softness of the painting. The artist had caught something of the soul. Something that should have been hidden from all mortal eyes. That was it, she thought, horrified. It was not the portrait of a beautiful woman. It was a portrait of destruction. She couldn't bear to look at the painting another instant. At once she knew why. She was staring at herself. This wasn't Karen's portrait. This was her portrait. It was as if she herself had died—and this image before her was all that remained. She stood there motionless. Her eyes could not leave the portrait.

He lit a cigarette and handed it to her, pulling her away from the painting to the sofa. She inhaled the smoke deeply, clinging to the slim white cylinder of tobacco, futilely hoping it would give her the support she needed. Neither of them spoke. Low strains of music whispered through the silence of the room. Her hand, as she put out the cigarette in the ashtray, was still trembling. He reached over and took her hand in his.

When he finally spoke his voice was low, the words were measured. "Why didn't you tell me she was your sister?" he said slowly. "Why?"

It was an inevitable question. She could only sit there and shake her head.

"Why, Edith?" he said again.

"How long have you known?" she said.

"Almost from the beginning."

"Did Alan . . . ?"

"No," he said. "No one had to tell me. You came back to find out what happened to her, didn't you?"

"Yes."

"And what did you discover?" The expression on his face was curiously impassive.

"Nothing," Edith said. "I found out nothing. Except what I read in the newspapers."

"Then why did you remain in New York? Why did you go to Lieutenant Gerard?"

She turned her face away. The words were caught in her throat.

"You see," he said. "I, also, wanted to find out about you. Everything that I could."

"You . . . you were quite successful," she managed to say.

"I've been thinking about you for a long time," he went on. "I haven't stopped thinking about you since the first moment I saw you."

She moved away from him. She walked over to the table and pulled out the interview she had prepared.

"I can leave this with you," she said. She fingered the papers nervously.

He walked over to her and took the papers from her hand and threw them on the table. "Never mind about that now," he said evenly.

She looked at him apprehensively. There was something about his eyes. The penetrating blue eyes had narrowed into angry steel bullets. The fear was creeping over her again. She was trapped. She wanted to run, hide, scream, but she could only stand there facing him. Hoping she could find a way out before it was too late.

"Why are you so afraid?" he asked her softly. "What are you afraid of?"

"This house," she murmured. "This room . . . I don't know." She was flustered. Groping for the right words.

"You're afraid of me, aren't you?" he said. "You don't have to be afraid." He touched her hair gently. "You're so much like her, Edith. So much like her. Enough to take her place."

"Don't, Mike."

"You must know how I feel about you. You knew that first night." He touched her face with his hand, and traced the outline of her features. She felt a strange thrill again tingling through her body. There was something about him that fascinated her, something she couldn't deny that was there every time he touched her. It enveloped her, hypnotized her.

He kissed her gently, possessively. "I want you," he murmured in her ear. "I always get what I want in time," he said. "And I have plenty of time. You're not ready yet. I know that. But you will be. And then . . ." He was kissing her again. She felt herself responding. She felt her control slowly breaking down again, crumbling in pieces.

"Please," she said, "please. This isn't right. I know it isn't."

"Why isn't it right? Who's to say what's right or wrong? He released her gently. "You're so much like her," he said huskily. "I want to possess you. I will possess you."

She moved away quickly and went to the fireplace. Karen was staring down at her with mocking eyes.

"She's here in this room. I can feel it," Edith said, her eyes on the portrait. "She's still your wife," she said softly. "As long as she still belongs to you, no one else can." She drew her eyes away, then walked toward the door.

"You're not ready to replace Karen," he said slowly. "Not yet, but . . . soon. Soon." He pulled a cord near the mantel. The butler entered the room.

"Philip," he said, "have the chauffeur drive Miss Weston to her apartment."

"Yes, sir."

Mike took her arm and led her to the foyer. The butler helped her on with her coat.

"I'll expect you Friday evening, the same time," Mike said impersonally.

She started to protest, but he broke in quickly, "I'll send the car for you. And . . ."

She paused at the door.

"The photographer won't be necessary."

She walked down to the iron gate, into the street. The black limousine was in front of the mansion waiting to take her home. Then just as she stepped inside a sickening image sprang before her. It was the sleek black car suddenly veering toward her at the crossing . . . and the remembered sound of someone's shrill scream piercing the night.

CHAPTER 24

It was nearly 1 A.M. when Edith returned to her apartment. She was tired. Horribly tired.

She switched on the lamp on the desk in the living room, and it illuminated a thin, haphazard assortment of the afternoon mail that she didn't have time to open before. She took off her coat, flung it on the couch, then sat down at the desk. She was exhausted, but her mind was racing through a montage of the evening.

She was caught now in the life she had always fantasized. She was caught in the crosscurrents of love, hate, revenge, suspicion, and maybe murder. She was wading deeper and deeper into Karen's life, into the mystery of Karen's death. She was trapped into it because of her own compulsion to live it. She knew that because of the way she responded to Mike Hewlitt in the perfumed, ivory bedroom. She knew too she had reached a point of no return, emotionally and physically. It was too late now. She had to go on even if she would be destroyed because of it.

She could no longer deny the Karen within her. It was breaking through in desire, fury, and rage. But it would have to break through. Only then could she finish that part off. The Karen in her must cease to exist so that Edith Weston could exist as the sum and substance of the whole. Only then could she know who she was.

But then . . . would then be too late? Too late to dream, to laugh, to love? Maybe there was a chance to stop right now. She could return to Paris. She would be safe there. Safe from everything.

She walked into the kitchen and picked up the telephone.

She touched the dial longingly. It was only 7 A.M. in Paris now. If she urged Maddy to return from Paris, there would be no meeting with Mike Hewlitt. She could blot Karen out of her existence, eliminate that menace that was compelling her to go on and on further into Karen's life. But she had a job to do. She gave Maddy her word. How could she let her down now? She turned away from the phone, and walked back to the living room.

She glanced at the mail on her desk. Circulars . . . magazines . . . bills. She stared at them sightlessly. Then she picked up a large square package. Thin . . . flat . . . wrapped in corrugated paper. She turned it over in her hands curiously. Her name and address were typed on a standard office label. There was no return address. Obviously, it had been hand-delivered. She loosened the wrapping with a letter opener, fumbled with paper, then pulled out a round black disc. It was a record.

She looked at the white and gold label in the center of the disc. Then she looked at it again. Then she stared at the label in horror. "Get Out of Town." She mouthed the title in silent terror. "Get Out of Town." She brought it over to the hi-fi machine and with trembling hands placed it on the turntable. She pressed a button and the arm of the machine dropped into the outer groove of the record. The music of the old pop song filled the room with an evil effluvium. She stared at the disc spinning around and around, her hands clenched to her mouth. Now the sounds of the words: "Get out of town . . . Before it's too late, my love . . . Get out of town . . ." The lyrics echoed and re-echoed through the apartment, mixing with the crazy, eerie strains of music.

She drew in her breath convulsively, and she screamed. And the scream was a dagger to pierce the music and kill it. She ran over to the machine, her face working, and snatched the record off. It broke into pieces in her hands. Her eyes filled with a terror that was beyond quelling. Whose macabre joke was this?

Tears smarted her eyes. She couldn't hold them back any longer. She sat down on a chair, the jagged parts of the record in her hands, and the tears flowed down her cheeks unchecked. She sat there for a long time sobbing, as if the unabashed flow would finally ease the tension, abate the fear.

She sighed. But the sigh was a shudder. The nameless, formless, terrifying enemy had won. She would have to . . . get out of town. Before it was too late . . . my love.

She went to the kitchenette and picked up the phone. Hastily, she dialed "O".

"I want to make a transatlantic call to the George V Hotel in Paris, operator, Miss Maddy Phillips."

She heard the voices and the dial tones over the transatlantic wires and her heart beat faster. Maddy will come back. Maddy must come back. Numb with trepidation, she heard the operator ask for Maddy Phillips, and she heard Maddy's voice far away in reply.

The operator cut back to her. "What is your number, please?"

"Regent 4-2323."

"Go ahead, please," the operator was saying to her. "Maddy Phillips is on the line."

"Maddy?" Edith steadied her voice.

"Hello . . . Hello? Edith?" Maddy's voice was faint, thin. "Can you hear me?" There were sounds on the line.

"Edith, can you hear me now?" Maddy was saying.

"Yes . . . yes. I can hear you."

"It's lucky you called this morning. I'm leaving for London this afternoon."

"I have something to tell you, Maddy."

"What did you say?" Edith heard Maddy signal the operator. "Operator . . . I can't hear anything."

There was another buzzing. "Just one moment, please," the operator broke in. "I'm trying to get you a clearer connection."

There was a long pause punctuated with static. "Go ahead, New York," the operator said. "Your party is still on the line."

"Edith, listen." Maddy's voice was clearer now. "I spoke to Stan and I'm leaving for London today." Maddy sounded strange. Out of control. "Stan . . . he . . . wants a divorce." Maddy's voice broke. "Can you hear me, Edith?"

"Maddy?" Edith said with alarm. "Are you all right, Maddy?"

"Yes . . . yes. What did you want to tell me?"

"Nothing . . . I . . . it was nothing. Listen, Maddy . . . when you see him maybe you can straighten it out."

"It's all settled." Maddy's voice sounded fainter. "Is everything all right? The Hewlitt campaign?"

"Yes . . . yes," Edith said quickly. "When will you be back?"

"Next week—Monday. If anybody tries to reach me . . . will you cover for me?"

"Yes, of course."

"You won't be able to reach me in London. I don't know where I'll stay yet."

"Okay . . . but if you need anything . . . will you call me, Maddy?"

"Yes . . . yes. Goodbye, Edith." Edith heard the click of the receiver on the other end of the line.

She slowly hung up the telephone. But the warning that was set to music was still swirling around in her mind. Get out of town before it's too late, my love . . . get out of town . . . before it's too late . . . on your mark, get set, get out of town . . .

CHAPTER 25

At four-thirty on Monday afternoon, Edith picked up the phone on her desk and dialed Pan American at Kennedy Airport.

"Could you tell me whether Flight 247 will arrive at six o'clock?" Edith said. "That's Pan American from Paris."

"Just one moment, please." There was a pause. "Flight 247, Pan American, is due as scheduled, six o'clock, ma'am."

"Thank you very much." Edith hung up the phone. And thank God, she said to herself. Mechanically she began to type out the Hewlitt profile again. His office. His career. His home. They were just words. A lot of words strung together. Empty, hollow words. The shock of the record . . . the sleek black car . . Karen's portrait . . . the shock of it all was still with her. Thank God, Maddy was coming back. Tonight. Six o'clock. The time she would retire from the account and let Maddy take over. She was through. Finished with Mike Hewlitt and his mausoleum and his human paintings. Maddy was her salvation. She never wanted to see Mike Hewlitt again. Guilty or innocent. The fatal fascination was more fatal than fascinating. She ought to go to Gerard. Show him the record. But she could visualize the futility of the scene. She could imagine his words. "We have no jurisdiction over what records people send in the mail, Miss Weston. Popular music isn't exactly in our line, Miss Weston. Go back to Paris, Miss Weston. A sleek black car trying to run you over? Wait for the red light, Miss Weston. Better still, get out of town—before it's too late, Miss Weston . . ."

She left the office and walked to her apartment. Before taking off her hat and coat, she picked up the phone and dialed Maddy's number. No answer. She waited another twenty minutes and dialed the number again. Still no answer.

Eleven o'clock. Edith dumped the cigarette butts in the ashtray into the wastepaper basket. She straightened the room again. Rearranged the books aimlessly. How much longer was Maddy going to take? Maybe something happened to her. What went on in London about the divorce? She remembered how Maddy sounded on the transatlantic phone call. Depressed. Frightened. Maybe something happened. Maybe Alan had heard from her. It was unlikely. Still, Alan would know what to do.

She spun Alan's number around on the dial.

"Alan," she said quickly. "It's me. Edith."

"Um?" he murmured drowsily.

"Please," she said urgently. "I'm terribly worried. It's about Maddy. Have you heard from her?"

"Maddy?" he repeated. "You wake me up to talk about Maddy? No, I haven't heard from Maddy, and besides, I don't want to."

"Alan," she pleaded. "I think something's wrong. The plane arrived five hours ago. Her phone doesn't answer. You've got to help me, Alan. I want to go to her apartment."

"You must be out of your mind."

"Alan." Edith's voice rose hysterically. "I'm sure something is wrong. You've got to meet me. I'm afraid to go alone."

"Okay," he said wearily. "Just give me a chance to get dressed. Ten minutes."

"I'll meet you there." She hung up the phone and put on her coat.

Outside she signaled a cab on Lexington Avenue, got in and gave the driver the address.

The cab sped along Lexington and turned left to Park Avenue. It drew up with a screech of tires at the curb of Eighty-first Street.

"You want the east side of Park, lady?"

Edith pulled a bill out of her bag. "It's okay." She waved off the change and rushed out of the cab.

"Thank you, lady!" the driver said, looking at the bill.

Alan was already in the lobby. "What's this all about?" he asked irritably.

Edith shook her head helplessly. "I'm sorry to get you out at this hour. But I didn't know what else to do," she said distractedly. "I know something's wrong."

"Did you check the airport?"

"Yes. She was on the plane, all right. She's supposed to be home now, but—"

"She could be at a hundred places."

"But . . . I called her in Paris. Her husband wants a divorce. She sounded . . . desperate."

"And what are we supposed to do about it?"

"Go up to her apartment."

"That's crazy! You can count me out."

"Please, Alan."

"What's your pitch, anyway? You couldn't wait to get her away so you could have Hewlitt all to yourself."

"I changed my mind," she said cryptically.

"No kidding," he replied laconically. "In that case, I'll stick around. Just to make sure."

They got into the elevator and pressed the button for the sixteenth floor. Alan followed her out of the elevator as she walked over to Maddy's apartment and rang the doorbell.

Alan held his head close to the door, but there was no sound from within. "Now what?"

"I've got the duplicate key," Edith said, fumbling with her bag.

Alan took the key from Edith. "You can't go barging into people's apartments. We'll get arrested for housebreaking."

Edith took the key back from him and inserted it into the lock.

Alan bowed low. "After you, my dear."

They stepped into the foyer, closing the door behind them. The apartment was dark. Alan moved his hand across the wall until he found the light switch. He snapped the light on and looked around the apartment. "It's empty," he said. "Now let's get out of here and have a drink."

"Look." She pointed to the floor. Two suitcases were standing there unopened. She turned on the lamp near a table.

"I'm going into the bedroom." Edith headed toward the hallway.

He stayed in the living room. He could hear her footsteps reach the bedroom door, then stop. Then he heard the doorknob turn. One second later he heard Edith's gasp. He raced to the bedroom. Edith was standing there frozen in the doorway. He looked past her, and lying on the bed with hair askew was the crumpled body of Madeline Phillips.

"Wait," Alan said firmly. "Just stand here." He walked over to the bed. He leaned his head close to Maddy's chest. "She's breathing." He leaned closer. Then he stood up. "She isn't dead. She's dead drunk. She just passed out."

"Drunk?" Edith wheeled around and stepped further into the

room. Now she could smell the pungent stale odor of alcohol. There was a half-empty bottle of scotch on the dresser. Maddy hadn't even waited to unpack.

"She started on this kick three years ago," Alan said.

"Borderline alcoholic?" Edith forced her eyes to the bed. Maddy's shattered form was hardly recognizable.

"She's already beyond the fringe. Didn't you know?"

Edith shook her head negatively. "Poor Maddy."

"And I suppose poor Maddy gives you another reason to change your mind?" he said tenuously.

"What do you mean?"

They moved into the living room. Alan picked up his coat. "You're going to stay on the job, aren't you?"

"Maddy's hardly capable of taking over. She can't keep her head above alcohol . . . even above water."

"She'll sleep it off," He started walking. "C'mon."

"I don't walk out on friends," Edith flared.

He picked up her coat and was putting it on her shoulders. "If you're her friend you ought to know the best thing we can do is get the hell out of here and forget it. You might injure her pride . . . if she has any left." He was already at the door.

"C'mon," he said quickly. They left the apartment in silence.

He pressed the elevator button. "So now you have another reason for staying . . . Maddy."

Another one?"

"Yes. The first is Mike Hewlitt. I heard around the agency that you've already seen his little mausoleum."

She studied the elevator door in front of her. "Maybe that mausoleum is really a monument to Karen's memory."

The elevator creaked to a stop and the door slid open quietly. They stepped inside and he pushed the button for the lobby.

He gave a short insidious laugh. "You wish you could believe that, don't you? Especially now. You must find him most attractive."

She stood there silently, her eyes turned away from him.

"And he's attracted to you," Alan went on. "He's got to be. You're just like Karen. Enough to replace her, maybe."

The elevator came to a halt. The door opened and they stepped into the lobby.

"Sometimes I feel sorry for him," she said in a low voice as they walked outside to the street. "How do I know he's guilty of anything?"

They stood at the corner facing each other. He stared at her quizzically. "You just feel sorry for him," he repeated with an edge to his voice. "But not enough to discontinue your pilgrimage to the pillars of truth." Then he glanced up and down Park Avenue searching for a taxi.

"What are you driving at now?" she asked him testily.

"Your strange motives" was his caustic reply. "If you were really that sorry, really exuding compassion, you'd stop seeing him. But you go on. Is it really your desire to find out about Karen? No . . . that would be too simple for such a complex woman as yourself. Could your motive possibly be love for Mike Hewlitt?" He shook his head negatively. "I dislike that word. Particularly in this context. So let's just stay with—attraction. Perhaps you're caught up irrevocably in your own script." He paused significantly. "I think you're out to land the Fabulous Face of the Decade."

"You're contemptible," she blurted with rage.

He raised his hand for the taxi on the other side of the street.

"Let me give you some advice," he continued imperviously. "I think he murdered your sister. You think so too. That makes it very inconvenient for you. So you have to find out the truth. You can't marry the man who murdered your sister." He looked at her narrowly. "But just remember this. Those wheels we started spinning . . . you weren't supposed to get caught up in them, Edith. So don't let your emotions get the best of you."

The taxi pulled up alongside them. He opened the door. "And now," he said shortly, "I'll see you home."

CHAPTER 26

"Darling." Maddy stood framed in the doorway of Edith's office. She was the essence of haute couture. The brown shapeless suit, the velvet draped cloche, the beige suede gloves crushed to the elbow. "Darling," she said again, carefully poised in the entrance to dramatize the effectiveness of the sum total of chic.

Edith got the message instantly. Maddy was giving a performance of the fashion editor just returned from abroad. It was, she thought, a rather pathetic performance. But at least it was live. Not like the drunken inertia of the night before.

"It was simply divine," Maddy said, beaming at her. Nowhere in her eyes was the slightest hint of any ordeal, or emotion. Apparently, she had recovered enough to present a mask to her public once more. If any words were going to puncture Maddy's last vestige of defense, Edith didn't want them to be her words.

"You look wonderful," Edith said, applying herself diligently to the role of captive audience. "And that"—she pointed to Maddy's dress—"is definitely a Dior." She tried to charge her voice with animation.

"A Pierre Rousse. His collection was superb. You'll drool when you see it," Maddy replied, swooping down into a chair. "Now tell me. Tell me everything."

Edith told her. She told about the visit to Mike's office. She described the evening at his mansion. The butler. The chauffeur. The rooms. She described in detail all the parts necessary for consumer consumption. And she eliminated the eerie record, the ominous car, and the ivory bedroom. Maddy registered ecstatic joy.

"You're doing a fabulous job. I knew you would. I wasn't worried for a second," she said. "Of course, Mike Hewlitt would be impressed with you, darling. What man could resist a beautiful woman?"

Edith flushed. "He was just being cooperative, that's all," she said quickly.

"Mike Hewlitt's no fool," Maddy replied, brushing off Edith's protests. She shook her bracelets. "I can hear the jangle of wedding bells already," she intoned coyly.

"Maybe you're just hearing things, Maddy," Edith said impatiently. The act was wearing a little thin, breaking at the seams.

"When do you meet again?" Maddy asked her, her voice dripping with intimate insinuation.

"I thought maybe you'd carry the ball, Maddy. Now that you're back." One last try, Edith thought. She tried to keep the despair, the urgency out of her voice.

Maddy patted her sleek dark hair beneath the brown velvet hat. "Not a chance, dear. I read your first article. If you do as well on the second . . . Mike Hewlitt will become a household word."

Edith managed the ghost of a smile.

"I saw Stan, you know," Maddy said. Then she added casually, "Like I told you before I left—I definitely decided to get a divorce."

Edith's eyebrows went up. Then hastily she covered her amazement. "I thought you might, Maddy," she said uneasily, wondering how much longer this performance could continue.

"I told you it would be the best thing for both of us," Maddy went on vivaciously. "The whole marriage was such a bore. Besides, I met the most divine man on the plane coming back. A New York lawyer. He was in Paris on business."

Edith took a slow beat before she spoke. It was impossible to sustain this act much longer. "Maybe that jangle of wedding bells you just heard was for you," Edith said cheerlessly.

She was getting the curious sensation that she had played this very scene many times before with Karen. Karen too could give a performance of pretense that rivaled the divine Sarah. And Edith would sit there applauding until it was over. Then she would have to reconstruct what happened, each painful sequence of some haphazard affair that Karen had embarked upon, and try to rationalize away the bitter consequences so that Karen would be fortified enough to start all over again. Well, she was finished being the captive audience.

"I thought surely you'd be in orbit by now," Maddy was saying. "The social orbit . . . via Mike Hewlitt."

"Let it drop, Maddy, will you?" Annoyance crept into Edith's voice.

Maddy spun her head around sharply. "What happened to you in the short span of ten days?"

"Perhaps I found out that orbit is another word for rat race," Edith said, bridling.

The artificial smile lingered precariously on Maddy's face. In another instant it would be gone. She was grappling to stick with the smooth performance, but the luster in her eyes gave way to a hard glassy stare. "You're turning into a message, girl," she retorted sharply. "Heaven spare me from that!"

Edith backed down a little. She had to remind herself this wasn't Karen. This was her boss. "Sorry, Maddy," she said contritely. "I didn't mean to stand on a reform platform. I was just telling you why I think it's time to retire."

"I know, sweetie," Maddy said pityingly. "But that Fisk "Time to Retire" slogan went out in the Thirties, remember?"

"I guess I'm just catching up with it now," Edith said, forcing a laugh.

Maddy shrugged her shoulders hopelessly. "And I thought you were going to take Manhattan by storm," she said with an undertone of sarcasm. She looked at her watch. "I'm meeting that dream man I told you about for lunch. And if this is part of the rat race . . . I'm going to start running right now."

And Maddy made a sweeping exit. It was all theater, every bit of it.

CHAPTER 27

This was the Friday evening of their next meeting. Edith drew the curtains apart and glanced down at the street below. In just a few more minutes she would step inside the luxurious interior of Mike Hewlitt's custom-built limousine, and be driven smoothly along the dark streets of the city to the town house on Sixty-eighth Street.

She still had time to change her mind, she told herself as she outlined the pattern of light rainfall outside the window with her fingers. An involuntary shudder ran through her body right to her fingertips where she held them against the window.

The night outside looked cold, friendless. She could stay here in the safe brightness of this room. It was her choice. She could remain here and try to shut out the night with its cold and wind and rain. But she would be alone. There was no one who could give her warmth enough to still the trembling inside her. There was no one close enough, tender enough, so there would be no night. There was no one who cared enough. Once . . . briefly, she thought it could have been Paul, and once even Alan. But each was just an interlude instead of an eternity. She wanted the eternity. Now she could settle for nothing less.

She gathered together the copy she had written, along with some memos from the Chanin agency about the profile. But even as she placed the assorted pages together in the envelope, she knew this time the manila folder was only a pretense.

She reached the street and the limousine was already there, waiting. The chauffeur held open the door and touched his forefinger to his cap. She stepped inside as Karen must have done hundreds of times before. But she felt none of the composure Karen must have felt. She only had a sense of aloneness.

As the car neared the mansion, the emotion sped to its height, and her sense of frightened solitude became increasingly apparent. No hand of support would stretch through the darkness toward her, no sign of help would be visible should she need it. She was sure now that this house held the answer to Karen's death.

Mike Hewlitt was at the door to greet her. Almost upon their entrance into the paneled library, the butler appeared with a tray of drinks. It was like the last time. Again she had the disquieting impression that every move she made was under the constant scrutiny of her host. He sat beside her and touched his glass to hers.

"It's been a long week," he said. "I was afraid you might not come this evening."

Her smile did not reach her eyes. "Why not?" she asked.

"Because I understand your editor is back from Paris. The agency called and asked me if I preferred having her work on this assignment instead. You know what my answer was."

She nodded silently.

"I told you," he said in a low voice, "that I wouldn't let you get away from me. I meant what I said."

Again she felt that intensity about him that frightened her, yet intrigued her so that she was helpless in its aura. It was like an octopus that controlled her every move in its embrace. She had the wisdom to lower her eyes to her drink and say nothing. But he wouldn't leave it at that.

"I think you are trying to get away," he went on softly. "I think you're afraid. Afraid of this house . . . afraid of me. And most of all . . . you're afraid of your own feelings." He downed his drink quickly and refilled his glass from a decanter on the table. "And I think that you're trying to forget with other men . . . just like she did."

"Trying to forget what?" Her voice was a mere whisper.

He stared beyond her. He was reliving an experience beyond this time and this place and the sound of her voice. "She . . . she was afraid. Afraid really of herself. So she tried to forget . . . with other men." He walked over to her and his hands gripped her shoulders so tightly that she winced from the pain. "But there won't be any other men. Not this time."

She twisted away from him. "There are no other men," she said, her face white with fear.

"Karen denied it too. But I knew . . . I always knew. And I know it now. He's trying to destroy my life, just the way he did before. He wants to take you away from me."

"Who?" she asked. "Who?" The question was barely audible.

"He and Karen . . . they thought I didn't know what was going on. Maybe she had others. But none of them mattered until Prescott." He clenched his hands into fists. "Prescott." He mouthed the name with ugliness. "I should have killed him."

Edith gasped. She sat there watching him, her eyes diluted with terror. It was the first time in her life she had seen a face, heard a voice that held so much hatred.

"She didn't want a divorce before that," he went on in the same bloodless way. "Then it all started to crumble. We both got caught in a vicious net of suspicion and lies and hate." His eyes shifted to the portrait over the fireplace. In the dimness of the room only blurred strokes of the painting were visible. "She was the only woman I ever wanted. I worshipped her. I adored her." With a sudden gesture he buried his face in his hands. Then he looked at Edith. "I would have given my life for her. I would give my life for you," he said slowly. "Because when I look at you . . . I see Karen."

Her eyes met his eyes and now hers softened briefly with a look of compassion. She was visibly shaken. She knew whatever he was once had ceased to exist with Karen's death. Whatever he was once had died with Karen and deep down he would never be the same again. He was merely going through the motions of life by trying to simulate the yesterdays.

"Why don't you let go of the past?" she said then, quietly, gently, she who could not let go of the past herself. "Your resentment of Alan . . . this house . . . that painting . . . her memory. Why don't you let go? Why?"

He moved back to the portrait again. "If she had only waited . . . I would have given her anything she wanted. Anything." He spoke with trembling emotion. "I would have given her a divorce. I would have learned how to accept life without her. But sometimes when you feel trapped . . . everything gets distorted." His voice broke. "I guess it nearly drove us out of our minds. Then suddenly there was one way out. One answer. One solution."

She held her breath with the question that was formed on her lips, the question that was about to break forth into sound at last. "What was the answer, the solution?" she whispered. Tell me, tell me now, she said silently. Please God, let me know the truth. If you are guilty, say that you killed her. If you are innocent . . . tell me what happened. Say it.

But all he said was: "I understood how Karen felt, but it was too late. Now all I can do is start again. Make it all the way it should have been and never was." His eyes were still fixed on the portrait.

"But how? How could you do that when Karen is . . . dead?" Her words cut through his memories to the present.

He turned and looked at her then as if he were seeing her for the first time. He drew her to him with his hands. He caressed her hair gently. "You look so much like her," he murmured. "You and I . . . we could have a whole world together."

"Don't, Mike. You're trying to create something that doesn't exist."

"Our world," he said, creating the enormity of his words with his voice. "No one could enter . . . no one could leave."

"Maybe you tried to live in that kind of a world with Karen. You can't shut out everything . . . everyone."

"It would be complete and perfect," he went on relentlessly.

"No, no," she said. "That way you cut off the tie line with life. You stifle it . . . you choke it to . . . death."

Then he put his arms around her. She was afraid to move, afraid to breathe. He drew her closer, closer, closer. Then all at once the fear and the magnetism and the compassion she felt toward him was fired into a single flame of desire. The intensity of her response matched his and she became engulfed with the passion, feverishly returning his kisses with her arms about him as he held her in his embrace.

"We can start all over again," he murmured in her ear. "I've waited so long for someone like you. I love you. I want you. I'll give you everything. Everything you want," he said with intensity.

"What did you give her, Mike?" she whispered. She must deny her feelings for him, she must fight against them, because she knew if she succumbed to him the shadow of Karen would always be there between them, haunting them, mocking them, snatching away their happiness. She could never live with love or live with peace as long as the question of Karen's death existed.

"I gave her the world," he said. "All that she wanted. Every wish . . . every whim." His mouth found her mouth again and he started to kiss her passionately, desperately.

She tried to move away, but his arms gripped her tighter and tighter. She managed to turn her head then and with a sobbing gasp she cried out, "Stop it! Stop it!"

Suddenly he released her and she ran to the sofa sobbing. At that moment she knew his world was the only one she wanted. But it was a world she could never have. It still belonged to Karen.

"What's wrong? What is it?" he asked in a low voice.

She moved from the sofa to the fireplace. She pressed the button that flooded the portrait with light. She stared at the magnificence of the image. The lifelike texture of the flesh. The smoldering green eyes. The flame of hair that surrounded the porcelain face. The picture sprang beyond the frame to include the past, present, and future.

"That's what's wrong," she cried in a voice charged with emotion and bitterness. It was a voice that she barely recognized as her own. "I'm sick and tired of being the stand-in for a memory!"

He stared at her uncomprehendingly. "I . . . I love you. I love you." He said it again and again.

But for her the repetition would not turn into truth. "You don't love me," she said. "You're trying to make Karen breathe again. With my face. My life. But you can't. You can't. Karen is dead. Dead. SHE'S DEAD!" The fact screamed out in the room.

He moved toward her slowly. "But you could never be another Karen," he said in a toneless voice.

She pressed her head against the paneled fireplace. The pounding within her was racing through every fiber in her body. "No," she said. And there was venom in her voice as she spoke. "I could never be another Karen. Because she was beyond replacement. Beyond even reality. You've made her into a beautiful dream. A fantasy that drifts gently by—always just out of reach."

He sat down next to her. "You would care for me the way she never did . . . never could. I know you would. I felt it . . . in your kiss. I saw it . . . in your eyes."

"Then what's driving you to do everything all over again just as if she were alive?" She uttered the words with passion, enough to force the answer from him.

"You don't understand," he said. "You just don't understand." He spoke like a man in a dream, vague mumbled words.

"I'm trying to," she said, pulling herself up to her feet as if the motion would bring her back to the solidity of reality. "God knows . . . I'm trying." She picked up a cigarette from the coffee table, steadying her voice. "Listen to me, please. If anything was wrong . . . if you're trying to hide something about Karen's death . . ."

He jerked his head up sharply and his eyes narrowed with distrust. "What made you say that?" he asked instantly.

She lit the cigarette and inhaled the smoke slowly. Then she said, "Because you're compelled to bring back the past . . . relive your life with Karen. Why, Mike? What are you trying to compensate for? WHY DO YOU FEEL SO GUILTY?"

The words hung in the air like a sword poised between them. His face went white. His mouth tightened. He moved his fingers together slowly, rubbing them against the palms of his hands. Silence enshrouded them with dark, unspoken insinuations that nudged their way into the stillness of the room.

Mike stood there staring at her. At that one moment it seemed as if this woman before him had stepped out of the painting to breathe again, speak again, taunt him, entice him with an exquisite femininity only to draw him close enough to beat him down with a cruel impact great enough to destroy him. At this moment, it seemed as if Karen was alive again.

He watched her now as she moved about the room. Her head was held high in that familiar gesture of imperiousness. She walked lithely, confidently. Her body moved gracefully. This could have been Karen walking about the room. Karen's body, Karen's face, Karen's manner. Karen, who took over the room completely. She had the power to enchant his senses, so that he desired her beyond any other. Nothing, no one else could exist in her presence. She could make him feel great, yet just at the moment of greatness she would strike, and the greatness would be crushed to insignificance. That was her power. Her cruel, destructive power. She could enchant, lure, entice all within her sphere until they were close enough to be destroyed. And then she would withdraw into her unbreakable shell, knowing that she had triumphed again. Yes, she knew her own power. She knew it well, and could use it at will. Karen was a sleek, sinuous cat about to spring on a wanted prey.

He remembered when he first met Karen, an eternity ago. But now the eternity had come alive with total recall. The unspoken promise in her eyes spread through her body and reached out to him with a rapport that could not be denied. Her kisses, her responses told him that she would be his until . . . until the time came when he reached out for her to fulfill all the spoken and unspoken words between them. Then came the recoil. She had sprung back, withdrawn, never to be possessed. She was the praying mantis who could only feed on a man's strength until that strength became a weakness. Then she left him to decay, rot, deteriorate in his own failure to have her. And that last night—Karen drank a toast to the future, knowing full well what the future would be. She sipped the liquid slowly, watching his reactions slyly. Yes, she already knew that she had triumphed. His consent to a divorce no longer mattered. Karen had found another way out.

Could Edith know, really know, what that way out was? Her words of accusation had shaken his senses. Why was Edith questioning the verdict of suicide? Was there something that Karen had told her that precipitated this suspicion? Karen was dead, but he had been a fool to think that he had finished with her. It was a supreme reincarnation. Now Karen was trying to destroy him with the implication that he had caused her death. What seeds of distrust had Karen implanted so that a scornful finger of accusation could brand him a murderer? Even from beyond the grave she had ordained that he should suffer with torturous feelings and self-doubts. He picked up his drink and swallowed it with difficulty. It took him a long while to find his voice, and when he did, his words came in a half-jumbled staccato. "Suppose . . . you tell me . . . what I am guilty of."

Edith forced herself to speak. She measured her words carefully. "If you keep on this way . . . it will only make things worse. Go to the police. I know it wasn't suicide. Tell them the truth." Tears wet her cheeks. Her heart seemed to stop beating. Her life was in his hands now. Let him finish it. She couldn't stand this living death a moment longer.

"The truth?" He looked at her oddly, then stood up and came toward her. "Do you know the truth? Do you think I killed her?"

He forced her to look into his eyes and she became frightened at what she saw. She was looking into the eyes of a man who already seemed to have died. Were they eyes incapable of feelings? Were they eyes that could have looked at murder and yet remain expressionless? A cold chill shook her body. He moved his hands over her body and touched her face. His voice returned momentarily to normal.

"You are the woman in that painting," he said softly. "That could be a painting of you. The portrait of Karen has come to life."

She shook her head mutely. She was so constricted with fear that she could not utter a sound. She seemed physically paralyzed.

"Yes," he went on, "not the stand-in for a memory. But . . . the memory itself." His hands traced her features carefully. "One and the same. The same, the same," he breathed lightly. His hands reached her throat. He fondled her neck, then the hands rested there. "I love you . . . I love you."

The hands seemed to press tighter, tighter. His voice sounded very far away, very faint. The room started to spin around like a crazy top. All at once everything went black, a shrouded, solid curtain of black.

Edith sank to the floor in a heap.

CHAPTER 28

The blackness was slowly dissolving. Edith thought she could hear a voice calling her name. But the voice was so far . . . so far. It was just a whisper echoing through smoky clouds. She felt as if she were being carried away on those soft clouds, far away into a wondrous place she already knew.

Now she was getting closer and closer and she could see the shape of a dome. It was an arena that rose high above the clouds and it was hanging in the sky. There was an audience below. Thousands of cheering spectators. And suddenly she found herself in a glass-enclosed booth trying to answer questions. It was a gigantic quiz show in outer space and she was the contestant. Everything was so gentle, so soft, and the motions of the people were so slow, so easy . . . as in a dream. She was struggling for answers. But her throat became constricted so that she could not speak, as if two powerful hands were gripping her throat tighter and tighter.

She leaned over the booth trying to find someone in the crowd below. The crowd screamed. There was a sudden silence. One false step and she would plunge downward into oblivion. But she didn't care. She was looking for someone who had the answers. All at once she saw the person standing across the orbit opposite her. It looked like . . . Karen. The same face. But this girl was smiling grotesquely. Her face was contorted into a frightening sneer. She was answering questions quickly, easily, confidently.

Edith called out to her. "Where is Karen?" she asked. "Are you Karen?" But the girl only looked at her and laughed. Edith moved closer to the rim of the circle. She held her arms out and called as loud as she could. "Karen . . . Karen . . . where is Karen?"

Edith could hear a voice calling her own name again. Someone was trying to stop the questions. Someone was shaking her shoulder. Edith felt she must get the answer. The voice was trying to stop her. She must call out again and get the answer quickly . . . very quickly, before anyone stopped her. The girl opposite her turned to go. She was stepping away from the orbit now, sinking slowly down among the evanescent clouds.

"Wait," Edith shouted. "Please, tell me . . . where is Karen?" she pleaded.

The girl with the red hair stopped now. Her dainty foot was just upon the outer rim of the arena. She turned around and faced Edith and smiled again. Then, without uttering a sound, she lifted her white arm high into the air, then moved it slowly down, pointing an outstretched finger toward Edith.

"No," Edith shouted. "I'm not Karen . . . not Karen . . . not Karen." Her voice was getting weaker and weaker, and she could hear her name being called louder and louder.

Someone was holding a glass of brandy to her lips. She tried to push the hand away but she didn't have the strength. Brandy was forced between her lips and she could feel the sweet heady liquid dropping down into her throat. She raised her hand to her forehead and felt a cool wet handkerchief on her brow. I must be dreaming, she thought. This must be all a dream. She tried to open her eyes and she could see now a faint blur of light. She flickered her eyelids, and moved the handkerchief away. That was better. She could see now. It was almost clear.

A voice said quietly, "Do you feel better now?"

She lifted herself up from the sofa. She was still in the room. It was the same room she was in before the dream. She knew she must leave quickly, get away from this room as fast as she could. Mike Hewlitt was sitting next to her holding a glass of brandy. He looked tense and worried; there were deep lines in his face. She must have dreamed the whole thing. It was just a dream.

"What happened?" she asked slowly, still dazed.

"You fainted. I was very worried about you."

She sat up on the sofa and managed to say, "I'm all right now."

"You must have had too much to drink," he said. "Would you like me to get you anything?"

"No . . . no, it's all right. If I could just get home . . ."

"Then let me have my car . . ."

"Please don't bother," she said, getting up. She pressed her hands to her forehead. "I can manage all right by myself. Thank you."

"You can't go home alone," he protested. "Not in this storm."

"The air will do me good. It isn't too far. Just a few blocks. I can walk." She picked up her bag and took out a comb and ran it rapidly through her hair.

"If you insist . . ."

"Yes. Please don't worry about me. I'm all right."

He followed her from the room to the foyer, then helped her on with her coat.

"It's a miserable night," he said. "Let me find you a taxi at least."

She stood at the door, afraid. The fear showing on her face.

"Don't go, Edith," he said. Now she was about to fade out of his life as strangely and suddenly as she had become a part of it.

"Don't go," he said again. But he knew the words were futile.

Her face tightened and he knew she was trying not to cry.

She was trying to control herself, but the tears came streaming down her face. "I . . . have to leave," she said. "Please . . . don't try to stop me." The words mixed with a sob.

He stood there with his hands hanging at his sides, and there wasn't anything more to say. She was right. She couldn't stay here like this, afraid of every move he made, every step he took. Fear was the only emotion she knew now. And somewhere in the maze, Karen was pulling the strings, dead or alive. Karen had come between them.

He wanted to go to her and put his arms gently around her and bury her face in his shoulder. He wanted to feel the wetness of her tears as he held her close, held her clinging to him. But they stood there apart with a whole world between them, Karen's world. He wanted to hold her so that moment would stop time itself, with nothing and no one else existing.

Finally he put his hand on the door and opened it. He didn't speak because all there was to say could never be said, and all he wanted to hear could never be heard. He felt then, as she turned to go, that a part of him had died a little.

A gust of wind and rain flung against her face as she left the house. She thought she heard him calling out to her as she ran down the steps along the path toward the iron gate. She didn't turn back. She pushed open the iron gate, stepped into the street, and headed toward Madison Avenue. Teeming rain poured into her hair, her face, all over her. She closed the collar of her black cloth coat, holding it against her throat. It was late. Nearly one o'clock in the morning. But she didn't care. At least it wasn't too late. She was still alive.

She didn't have to run now. It would have seemed incongruous with the lonely rain-soaked night, the emptiness of the streets. There were no lingering cabs waiting for a fare. Who was there to watch her if she ran, to listen if she screamed? She glanced back over her shoulder furtively, looking into the watery shadows. She thought someone was following her. There was a sound of footsteps mixed with the beating of rain on the pavement behind her. A man was lurking there. He came close behind her. She drew a breath. Then the man passed her slowly, walking on. Just another stranger in the night, like herself.

She hurried on. She waited on the curb for the green light, feeling foolish, because there were no cars to block her way. Then she crossed with the signal and headed toward Lexington Avenue. The wind was raging around her now, and the cold raindrops splashed down against her face, on her coat, splattering against the pavement. The rain will turn to ice, she thought, it's so cold, so wet. She shivered. Just then at the corner she saw a policeman pounding his beat. She had a sudden urge to go to him and tell him what happened, tell him that she was afraid, afraid for her life. But he would ask questions. He would think she was crazy running up to him in the darkness with the wind howling, to tell him that someone tried to strangle her. Or was it just sheer panic, a nightmare?

The tears were still wetting her face, mixing with the rain. She could cry alone now because she had left him and she was afraid, but still she wanted him. She knew she would never see Mike again, and that tore at her insides because she knew she could love him if all of this hadn't existed. But how could she love a murderer?

Suddenly she stopped in the middle of the street. But she was in love with him. She could no longer deny it.

She kept hearing his voice, seeing his face, his haunted eyes, the look of hurt and anguish. The rain was pouring down harder now in a sudden gush of renewed strength. She just stood there and let it beat down on her. Then she started to laugh and sob all at once. Mike hadn't tried to kill her. She had to go back to him. He needed her. He hadn't tried to kill her. It was panic. That's why she fainted. Panic. Even in the rain and wind and the storm she could feel his arms around her, she could hear his voice saying over and over again that he loved her, that he wanted her. Even in the cold she could feel his warmth. She wasn't alone anymore. She wanted him and because of her fear she had almost run away. She wanted him on any terms, even if she had to become the substitute, the stand-in for a memory. Even if he was guilty. She didn't care anymore. She only cared about him. She was going back to him.

She started walking uptown. The torrent of rain was beginning to stop and now it was falling with a consistent, steady lightness. She knew if she could be with him again that somewhere in the nightmares, the dreams, and the realities, they could find the answers together.

The Hewlitt mansion loomed before her once again. She ran past the open iron gate up the narrow path that led to the front doors. She pressed the white button and heard the soft answering chimes within. The doors opened. Mike was standing there on the threshold. She walked slowly into the white marble foyer and he closed the doors after her. She was drenched through to the skin . . . her clothes and her hair wet and shining with the rain. She stood there helplessly, not knowing what to say or how to say it. But she knew he understood. She could see the knowing in his face, the desire in his eyes. She stepped toward him and with that gesture her defenses were gone, no longer necessary. She was no longer afraid. Fear was replaced by compassion. In a quick moment she felt his arms crushing her to him.

CHAPTER 29

It was subdued and quiet in the bedroom. Just fragments of the cold December night peered through. Narrow slits of exposed windows revealed the reflection of streetlights that lingered on the glass. Edith focused her eyes on the small piece of night outside.

Here the sounds of night could not be heard . . . the sounds of winds that filled the darkness, the sound of a child crying, the sound of cars grinding their way through the city . . . She was glad not to be out there, a part of it.

She felt so close to him, so very close that she knew the magic must endure. Magic and endurance—they were two qualities that she had been forced to accept as incompatible, implacably hostile toward each other. But tonight for the first time she felt that the magic could be the eternity.

He switched on the lamp next to the bed and the soft shaft of light illuminated the room. It was such a large bedroom, such a vast bed. In the darkness before she couldn't see the mahogany walls and the terrace outside that stretched along a wall of windows that was almost concealed by massive folds of soft white curtains.

He reached for the cigarettes on the night table and lit one for her. Then he asked suddenly, "Why did you come back tonight, Edith?"

The answer now seemed inevitable. "Because I love you," she said in a low voice.

"Even though you thought I killed her?" He watched the stream of smoke as it coiled in front of him.

Her voice had a choked sound. "Yes." The sound of the word mixed with a sob.

"But why me?" he asked quietly.

She hesitated. "It was the letter. She wrote to me in Paris just before she died. There was another man. She was going to leave you and marry someone else. They would be in Paris on their honeymoon the end of December."

Mike said, "And the man?"

Edith shook her head. "She didn't tell me his name. The letter came just after she died. It didn't make sense. Why would she kill herself if she wrote me that letter? So I left Paris as soon as I could. I showed the letter to the police. Lieutenant Gerard. His feelings confirmed my suspicions about the suicide verdict, but he said there was nothing he could do. It wasn't proof. The case was closed."

"So you decided to find out for yourself."

"I had to, Mike. I had to try." She paused. "I didn't know then I was going to fall in love with you."

He got up and walked back and forth across the room, then stood opposite her, leaning against a table. "I want you to listen," he said in measured words. "I want you to try to understand."

"You and I, Edith," he said slowly, "had one thing in common in the beginning. The mutual pursuit of Karen." He sat down in a chair. "There were times when I began to think of you as Karen not only because of the physical similarity but because I wanted to replace her." He paused to put out his cigarette.

She sat there listening, her hands clenched tightly on the coverlet.

"Once I worshipped her, adored her. I honestly believed that life was unbearable without her," he went on. "I tried to relive those emotions to forget the other ones. That's why my home looked like a monument to a memory. It was. Because I was trying to hide the fact from the world and myself that it was in reality a monument to *hate*."

"You . . . you hated Karen?" She gasped the words.

"It doesn't seem possible, does it, when I did everything I could to re-create my life with Karen. I even tried to make you into her replacement so I could carry my denial of the truth even further. But it didn't work, Edith. It didn't work because of you. You are the portrait of Karen. Yes, the face is the same. But the soul is different. You are a woman. She was a devil!"

The exquisite painting seemed to spring into Edith's eyes. She could see the lovely, breathtaking face . . . the softness . . . the beauty . . . and then beyond that . . . the strange expression of cruelty that permeated the canvas. Would it ever fade into oblivion?

"Did you really know Karen?" he asked her. "People would find it hard to believe the truth. Karen was a potent force of destruction," he said slowly and clearly. "Her life was a continuing play . . . a series of incomparable scenes. She was the only star, the only performer. She was always onstage. But she had only contempt for her audience. Her only object was to destroy those who paid her homage. This was her triumph."

Edith said, "I knew her triumphs only too well."

"But she never attained success," Mike said bitterly, "because as a human being she was a failure. And she wanted to drag all within her reach down to the bottom with her."

"You make her sound almost . . . inhuman."

"She was inhuman. I was glad when she died." Mike breathed out the words. "Glad. I . . . hated . . . Karen. Can you understand that?" The words wrenched themselves out of him, and then there was silence.

Somewhere in the room a clock ticked monotonously in the quiet that followed. Then Mike went to the window and raised it a bit, letting a touch of night enter the room. A sheet of wind curled the curtains back and forth, then loitered to cool the room and mingle with the silence and the ticking of the clock. Edith shivered.

"Mike . . ." she said with difficulty. "Then you . . . killed her? You destroyed her because you hated her?" She couldn't keep the despair out of her voice.

"Yes, I hated her," he replied. "Anyone can hate. Only fools have no hatred inside of them," he said to her. "Hatred is an insidious emotion only when it is stifled, denied. Hatred is a dark thing that can breed itself only in dark places. In the guts of a man, in his stomach, in his heart. It feeds in blackness where it cannot be seen. But hate, like love, has its place in each soul." He paused. "I too am entitled to hate. But my hatred became so enormous, so strong that there was room for nothing else inside of me."

Edith looked at him. The question was too painful. But she had to ask it again. "You killed her? It was you?"

He didn't answer. He walked around the room haphazardly and kept on talking.

"The misery," he said, "the loneliness of living only with hate. I had it. Finally I was willing to let her go. But it was too late."

"Then you did kill her," she persisted. "Why did it have to be you, Mike? Why?"

"I loved her," he said, "in the beginning. Yes, I knew what she was like. Shining, glittering, beautiful. Spoiled, cruel. But I didn't care. To me that was part of the fascination. Someone who wasn't quite attainable. The first woman I wanted that I couldn't really have. So I married her. That way I thought I could possess her forever. But I was wrong, of course. Marriage doesn't change anything. It merely formalizes. Marriage is just a gesture that underscores the truth with legality. I was married to loneliness. I always have been. But I didn't realize . . . I didn't know I was asking for destruction."

Edith stared at him. "But Karen is the one who was destroyed," she said.

"Yes," he answered. "Karen was destroyed." His short laugh was mirthless. "It was the ultimate irony of all. That last night we were having a terrible argument. We were in the library . . ."

She listened to his words, words that spilled out as if they had been bottled tightly, then suddenly uncorked. They spurted out in torrents, a wave that filled the place so that it was no longer a room but another dimension in space where the past was re-created and made a part of the present once again.

CHAPTER 30

The scene was moving back in time and space to a time when the dead was the living. When Mike and Karen were man and wife.

"We were married for eight years. The last three were a living hell. I knew about the other men. I waited for the time it would stop, but it never did. Nothing seemed to satisfy her. And no one. I thought someday it would be different and I waited. Then she met Alan Prescott. I thought it would pass like the rest. But this time it was different. This time she asked me for a divorce."

The expression in his eyes hardened. She stared, almost hypnotized by the sudden savagery of his voice that was incongruous with his pale, impassive face.

"I told her I would never consent to a divorce. I told her that," he went on, "many times before that night in the library. It wasn't the first argument we had about it. But I didn't know it was going to be the last. I can see her now with her eyes taunting me, the venomous expression on her face. She said to me, 'Where is your pride, Mike? The great Mike Hewlitt, the famous industrialist . . . living with a woman who hates him?'"

Now Edith could see the luxurious paneled library and the two of them standing there facing each other, hating each other. Karen, beautiful, flaunting her sinuous body, imperious and triumphant, because she knew no one would ever possess her, and all men wanted to. And Mike, desirous beyond reason, beyond pride, pleading with her to stay with him, believing that he worshipped her.

"I gave her everything," Mike said, his voice trembling. "I told her that. She threw her head back and laughed and said that she had to take me with it and that was too much for anyone. I reminded her that we were in love once, in the beginning. She looked at me with contempt. I'll never forget her words.

"'Do you think I married you because I loved you!' she said. 'Do you really think that?'

"Then I asked her why she married me.

" 'It's obvious,' she said. 'I married you for money. For the things I never had. And I'm going to divorce you for the same reason.'

"I told her to get a divorce. But she wouldn't get my money. She had known that for a long time. She knew she had no grounds, she couldn't even think of any legal grounds. Then she started to threaten me. She'd smear my name, ruin my reputation. My photograph would be splashed across every newspaper in the country. I told her no one would believe her.

" 'Won't they?' she said strangely. 'I plan to sue you for divorce in New York City.'

" 'On what grounds?' I asked her.

" 'Adultery, of course,' she said. 'There are ways to manufacture evidence. You aren't going to want that kind of publicity. Not Mike Hewlitt. I'll make it a field day for the newspapers.'

"I looked at her calmly. 'If blackmail is your little scheme . . . it just won't work, Karen. You won't get a cent.'

" 'Think what this could do to the Hewlitt name,' she said.

" 'If you want to take this to court, I'll prove you're guilty of perjury. Go ahead, Karen, sue me for divorce.'

"She knew then I meant what I said. It was a cheap trick. And it didn't work.

"She seemed to reconsider for a moment. Then she smiled in a curious way and suddenly said, 'Very well, Mike. Then we'll go on this way.'

" 'There are no locks on the doors,' I reminded her.

" 'You'd like me to walk out, wouldn't you?' she sneered. 'Then you could charge me with desertion. But I'm staying, Mike. Because that wouldn't fit into my plans at all.' "

Mike had stopped talking. His face turned pale, haunted. The room was filled with the painful memories that had come alive to taunt him. It seemed so painful that he no longer had the strength to go on.

"I thought she wanted money," he said unsteadily. "Money to subsidize her affair with Alan. I thought maybe she had finally fallen in love. What a fool I was. Little did I know that Karen could love no one but herself." He stared at the table, the room, seeing nothing except the memories.

"We ate dinner that night in complete silence. All I could think about was the miserable failure of my marriage, and the grief she had caused me. How could I have been so blind . . . so stupid? I wished . . . yes, I wished that she was . . . dead. Finally Karen spoke.

" 'I think we should at least drink a toast to our future together,' she said sarcastically.

"She was going on with the farce. She got up from the table and took a wine decanter from the sideboard. She poured out two drinks and brought them back to the table.

" 'Well, drink up, Mike,' she said, holding up her glass. 'To the perfect marriage.'

"I hardly knew what she was saying. She started to sip the wine, then the phone rang. It was Alan Prescott. The butler asked if she wished him to call back after dinner. But she sprung from the table and hurried to the foyer to take the call. I could hear some of the conversation from the dining room.

"She was telling him she had to see him. I thought she was planning to run away with him. But then I no longer cared what she did with her life. I didn't want any part of it, nor did I intend to pay for it if I had to hire every legal expert in the country.

"The butler walked back into the room. He asked me if he should serve the dessert . . . if Mrs. Hewlitt was going to finish her dinner. He started to clear the table, then accidentally spilled her glass of wine. He seemed flustered and upset. I'm sure the servants knew what was going on. I told him to give her my glass of wine, and he did so, setting it down on the table before her. Karen came back into the room.

"She stared at the empty glass beside me and said, 'You should have waited, Mike. We could have had our little toast together.'

"She raised the glass to her lips and said, 'To a perfect future!'

"She drank the wine quickly and stood up from the table. She went upstairs to her room without saying another word.

"I left the house. I felt as if I couldn't stay there another second. I walked the streets for hours trying to clear my mind. She knew I hated publicity, how humiliating it would be to see the Hewlitt name smeared across the newspapers, and the stares and whispers of people who knew me. She had gone to every extreme to extract a huge sum of money from me. But this time she wasn't going to get what she wanted.

"I returned to the house. It was late, after two, and it was dark and quiet. I got into bed. Karen long ago had refused to share the same room with me. I tried to sleep, but I could only lie awake with living nightmares. I guess I hoped that by not giving her the divorce things might change, might be different. But even as I thought this, I realized it would never be any different. She hated me. Even from the start. Just the way I now had begun to hate her. She only wanted my money. I had to face it and let her go. I finally decided the only thing to do was to consent to a divorce. Whatever it cost it would be better than this. I would arrange for a quiet divorce, with no publicity, no notoriety. She could have her way as always. Karen had won again. I dozed off about five in the morning. When I awoke, it was nine o'clock. I wanted to tell her as soon as possible. Get it over with once and for all. I went to her bedroom door and knocked. There was no answer. Karen was usually an early riser. I knocked again, then I tried the handle. The door was locked.

"I called out her name. There was no answer. Then I began to get worried. I went downstairs and asked her maid if she had left the house earlier. But she said that Mrs. Hewlitt was still asleep. Taking the master key, I went back to her bedroom and opened the door.

"She was across the bed, sprawled out, still dressed in the clothes she had worn the night before at dinner. I went over to her. I thought maybe she had been drinking. I leaned closer. She wasn't breathing. It was horrible. She was dead. Karen was dead. I lifted her arm and it dropped lifelessly to her side. How? Why? Was it my fault? I tried not to panic. But all I could think of was that she killed herself because of me. Then I noticed the white sheet of paper on the floor next to the bed. It was a note scrawled in her handwriting. I leaned over to pick it up and started to read the words that became a blur before my eyes. I couldn't believe what I was reading. Then I read it over again, slowly, carefully. I remember every word just as I read it then. I went over it a dozen times. The police have it now, but I'll always remember her words of life and death. It was a lamentably insignificant message for dying, when her living contained so much dramatics.

"She wrote: 'I cannot go on like this any longer with you. Our life together has no meaning. I am sick and tired of it all. It's much better this way for both of us.' That was all there was to it."

He looked at Edith, and he was as pale as death itself. Edith stared back at him, horrified. She had died a thousand deaths with him as he relived the memory. So Karen had taken poison by her own hand.

When Edith finally spoke, her voice came through as in a dream, soft and far away.

"How she must have suffered," Edith murmured. "To take her own life, to blot it all out that way. How she must have suffered to commit suicide."

There was a silence for a moment. Then, when Mike spoke, Edith thought this surely must be part of the dream too.

"Karen didn't commit suicide," Mike said evenly and calmly.

Edith's eyes dilated. "But you just . . . you just told me what was in the suicide note."

"It wasn't her suicide note," she heard him say.

"What do you mean?"

"It was . . . mine," he said slowly. "Mine. The note was intended to be found next to my body. Not hers."

The room came back into focus. She could see the mahogany walls now, sharp and clear, and the furniture, and soft carpeting.

He walked over to an antique desk and unlocked a drawer. She saw a sheet of white paper in his hand and then he came toward her and held it out to her. She took the paper from him and held it up to the light. Her eyes scanned the page with astonishment. "This one was locked in her bureau drawer," Mike was saying.

Edith drew her eyes from the page and gasped. "But it's the same thing, Mike. It says the same thing except it's written on a typewriter with your name signed to it. I don't understand. What does it mean?"

"Yes, this one is typed," Mike was saying. "On my typewriter. The words are the same. But my name is on this. The other one had no signature. This note is signed in my handwriting. She had forged my signature exactly. Suddenly it made sense. She intended to kill *me*. It was carefully planned before the argument. My suicide note on the scrap of paper which the police have was just a rough draft that she had already composed. She copied it over on this paper with my typewriter. Then she forged my name. The note you're reading now was supposed to be found next to my body. The poison in the wineglass—it was meant for me. She drank my glass by mistake. She had it all figured out . . . the money she would inherit . . . the murder that would look like suicide . . . except for the last detail. She drank from the wrong glass. Karen never had a chance to use this suicide note. She killed herself accidentally," he said. "Karen's death was accidental."

It was an accident. Mike was innocent. The Hewlitt mansion loomed in Edith's mind . . . the magnificent lawn and the iron gate all designed with thick shrubbery and spreading trees so that no eyes could penetrate its secrets. She conjured up once again the luxurious library with the portrait of Karen hung above the fireplace . . . and the delicate white bedroom where Karen's body lay lifeless, still, and the suicide note on the floor. It was the final, tragic irony that Karen, who had everything she ever wanted, had become her own victim. It was a modern Greek tragedy with the destroyer becoming the destroyed, the perpetrator of evil becoming the protagonist of her own death. And Mike had sustained the whole fabricated love fable so that the world would never know the truth. He had mourned as a lover would have mourned. He had presumably kept his home as a shrine for his beloved, but the shrine was merely a camouflage for the truth. Why, then, did he live this lie? Why, then, did he protect Karen even in death? The question was forming on her lips. He started to speak again.

"You must be wondering," he said, "why I kept silent. Why no one ever knew the truth—how much she hated me. Enough to try to kill me."

"You told no one?"

"That must seem strange to you," he replied," after all that she did to me. She humiliated me, taunted me with things I can never speak about, not even now. She carried on love affairs with men who knew me, yet with all of that I still wanted to protect her name. Why? Because I had one thing left that could never be destroyed, not even by Karen. I had my pride. If the truth were known, can you possibly imagine the repercussions? The name of Hewlitt would be on everyone's lips. My enemies would triumph in my debasement. No, I couldn't stand that." He drew himself up as he spoke. "I still had my pride. She couldn't destroy that. Not if I remained silent."

"But what about the police? Surely they—"

"The police? It was simple. I hid the typewritten suicide note that gave away the truth," he said. "I knew they would check Karen's writing that was on the paper next to her body, and accept what they had found as an authentic suicide note. How could they know it was meant for me? Oh, they made a very careful check on everything. Lieutenant Gerard is not to be underestimated. They traced the poison in her body, and in the glass. They even found the drugstore where she had purchased it. Everything proved it to be a case of suicide. During the inquest I had a sort of intuition that Gerard guessed the truth. But there were no facts to go on. Karen was dead. Poisoned by her own hand. But her death was accidental. She had no intention of committing suicide. Gerard never said anything if he did suspect what really happened. The case was closed."

"So you kept silent."

"Wouldn't you have done the same?" he asked her. "Karen had paid with her life for the crime she wanted to commit."

She put out her hands and pulled him down to her, and held his head in her arms. "Oh, Mike," she whispered. "Mike. I love you. We'll forget the past. Wipe out the whole thing as if it never happened. We can start all over again . . . and make it the way it should have been."

"I tried to make you into the Karen that should have been," he said. "Because I loved her in the beginning. But the past is unalterable, final. You're not a part of that past anymore, Edith. For that I'm glad. I want you the way you are. Just Edith. The past belongs to Karen. The present belongs to you. The future belongs to us."

Edith. Just Edith Weston at last, she told herself. She had waited a long time for those words. A lifetime.

CHAPTER 31

Two men stared at her as she opened the door of the office. Edith paused in the doorway.

Lieutenant Gerard motioned toward a chair. "We were expecting you, Miss Weston. This is Detective Regan."

The tall dark man in the brown suit moved forward a step, his eyes never leaving her face. "How do you do, Miss Weston," he said pleasantly.

"I wanted Regan to take a good look at you, Miss Weston," Gerard explained. "The next time he tries to locate you, at least he'll be able to place the face." Gerard turned to the detective. "Okay, Bill."

Regan nodded, then left the office.

"What's this all about?" Edith sat down, looking toward the door Regan had just closed after him.

"You disappeared over the weekend," Gerard told her. "I was getting a little concerned about you."

Her eyebrows went up. "A little concerned? Then why the detective, Lieutenant Gerard?"

"Now, Miss Weston," Gerard interrupted soothingly. "Of course I knew you would get here sooner or later. But . . ."

Edith twisted her handbag in her fingers nervously. "But you were going to make sure I got here sooner. What was so urgent?"

"Where were you, may I ask?" Gerard inquired politely.

"Walking," she said. "Just walking."

"And where were you last night?"

"Walking," she said abruptly.

Gerard puffed gently on his cigar. "We've been trying to locate you since Saturday morning. This is Monday night. Your whereabouts were unknown until you showed up at your office this morning. I was quite relieved to hear your voice on the phone this afternoon." Then he added mildly, "We thought you might have run into some sort of difficulty."

"I'm sorry you went to all that trouble," Edith said. "But at the moment I'm very healthy, Lieutenant. I can take care of myself."

"Saturday, Saturday night, Sunday, Sunday night," Gerard mused. "That was some walk." He shook his head. "And with all that rain too. Hardly the weekend for a stroll," he said softly.

"Nobody told you to check up on me," Edith flared.

Gerard dropped his glance as he placed his cigar in the ashtray. Then he folded his hands on the desk.

"No." He raised his eyes toward her. "Nobody told me, but my insomnia started to kick up again."

"What's that supposed to mean this time . . . I'm the next suspect?"

"No. The next victim. You were with Mike Hewlitt, weren't you?" It was a rhetorical question.

She twisted her handbag again, then held it tightly on her lap trying to compose herself. "What if I was?"

"In his home?" Gerard asked. "Did you happen to tell him about the letter Karen wrote you in Paris before she died?"

"Yes, I told him." Edith paused. "What difference does it make?"

Gerard cleared his throat, then adjusted his voice to an official monotone. "We've decided to reopen the Hewlitt case."

Edith stared at him in astonishment. "Reopen the Hewlitt case?"

"We have reason now to suspect that Mike Hewlitt murdered his wife."

Edith grappled with the words she just heard. She was trying to think lucidly and unemotionally. She closed her eyes tightly to shut out the panic she felt. But she only had a blurred vision of newspaper headlines splashed across the front page. "Famous industrialist murders his wife. Mike Hewlitt found guilty of murder." The pain was in her heart again. She could hardly breathe as she spoke.

"It isn't possible," she said. "It just isn't possible. I know it isn't true."

Gerard had moved from the desk. The file of the Hewlitt case was in his hand. "That's why we were so anxious about you, Miss Weston. I had to reach you to tell you this because I had a pretty good idea where you were. If our suspicions are correct, your life is in jeopardy. I didn't want a dead victim to prove our assumption. It was urgent that I warn you to keep away from him."

"But you said you need proof. You said the case was closed. What made you change your mind?"

He drew an envelope from the folder and held it up. "This letter," he said. "The one she wrote you in Paris. And"—he took a scrap of white paper from the file—"and this suicide note."

"But you knew all of this."

Gerard sat down at his desk again, holding the letter and the suicide note in his hands. His face was grim as he shifted in his chair. "I knew it, but I never put it together," he said. "The paper . . . the writing paper she used in her letter to you—thick, expensive paper. The Tiffany imprint is on the back flap of the envelope. The paper she used for the suicide note—take a look at it." He held it up again. "Cheap notepaper, hastily scrawled writing. Why did she use cheap notepaper? Where did she get it from? There was no other paper like this in the house."

"But it is her handwriting," Edith said in a low voice. "Anyone can see that."

"Sure. It's her handwriting, all right. But it isn't her suicide note."

Edith swallowed hard. If Gerard guessed the truth, if he deduced what really happened, how did he reach the conclusion that Mike was guilty? "Then . . . then whose is it?" Edith stammered.

"It isn't a suicide note at all," Gerard said concisely. "Listen to the words she wrote. Listen carefully: 'I cannot go on like this any longer with you. Our life together has no meaning. I am sick and tired of it all. It's much better this way for both of us.'" Gerard looked up from the page. "She wrote this note more than two weeks before she died. We traced the paper. It's from the Forum of the Twelve Caesars, a restaurant she frequented. One of the waiters recalled giving Mrs. Hewlitt a piece of paper from his notebook while she was dining there one night with a man we have identified —Alan Prescott. We checked with Prescott. We didn't tell him what we suspected, but Prescott confirmed that Mrs. Hewlitt was going to leave her husband that night because he wouldn't consent to a divorce. He confirmed the fact that she wrote this note at the table, then put it in her bag. She told Prescott she was going to a hotel that night. Right after dinner Prescott took her home. His story checks. That same night she moved into the Plaza Hotel."

"But she was still living with her husband when she died."

"It wasn't the first time she walked out on him," Gerard said. "She stayed at the Plaza for five days, then returned home. We think Hewlitt somehow found the note and kept it for later use. That note was going to look like her suicide note. He then set up his plan for murder. He asked Karen to buy the hypo at the druggist's to establish the fact that she bought it herself. The night he poisoned her he placed the note next to the body." Gerard sat there watching his gray smoke rings drift silently upward. "We're going to take Hewlitt in for questioning. We've already put a watch on him. He won't get away from us this time."

It's all gone up in smoke, Edith thought desperately. Her life with Mike, the future they planned together . . . it was gone. She was on a treadmill that moved quickly to nowhere. Should she tell Gerard what she knew or should she warn Mike first? Then at last she spoke, quietly, slowly.

"Everything isn't always fact or tangible evidence," she said. "You told me that yourself once. There may be something else you've overlooked."

"Is there?" he shot back at her. "You were with him this weekend. Perhaps you can tell me what I've overlooked."

Edith felt her face redden. "I don't know," she said. She looked away from him, focusing her eyes on the burning ash of the cigar butt resting on the ashtray. It was better to admit nothing, she thought. Say nothing. She prayed that Mike would be able to clear himself with the copy of the suicide note that had his name forged on it. She moved her eyes about the small office haphazardly. She didn't speak. What else could she say? From outside the window she could hear the hum, then the sudden zooming of a jet plane that passed overhead, darting through space, and then the sound was gone. The wind started to brush against the glass pane behind Gerard's desk, carrying some fallen leaves that clung briefly to the window, then were swept away. Night had closed in. She was tired now. Tired of questions she could not answer . . . tired of decisions she was unable to make. It was a gloomy, hapless scene, the two of them there in the desolate office discussing murder and attempted murder and suicide and no one able to grasp at anything concrete. Just a lot of words bandied back and forth across the room. Words that were hollow, accusative, and speculative that added up only to Mike's guilt. She wanted to leave this place, this room, these words. She wanted to leave all of it once and for all.

She stood up now, still clutching her bag tightly. Her face was drawn and there was a line between her brows. She was beaten down from the uselessness of it all, the frustrations, and above all the fear that Gerard's deductions were correct. Mike could have murdered Karen. The story he told her could have been mere fabrication. It could have been his car that tried to kill her . . . his record that spun the warning. It was a terrifying idea, and quite possibly, the truth.

She moved toward the door. "May I go?" she asked Gerard. "Or am I being held for questioning also?"

"You may go, Miss Weston. Certainly. I merely felt it was my duty to warn you . . ." His voice trailed off behind the swirling smoke.

She paused at the door. The letter Mike had shown her, the typewritten version of Karen's alleged suicide note, flashed before her. She visualized the small black printed letters . . . the watermarks on the paper as she had held it up to the light in Mike's bedroom Friday night. Why did she keep thinking about it from the moment she held it in her hand? Why did she keep seeing it over and over again?

Suddenly . . . the answer screamed out at her. She nodded to Gerard and left the office quickly.

CHAPTER 32

A drugstore was around the corner. She ordered black coffee and sipped it slowly, trying to evaluate the reasons for Gerard's latest symptoms of insomnia. One thing was clearly evident. Her life was in danger. The police had put the official stamp on that when they reopened the Hewlitt case. The question . . . the probing . . . the skeletons were no longer under cover. Gerard was moving in fast. Fear would make the guilty move even faster. She had to be very cautious. She knew she could get evidence that would protect Mike. She also knew that same evidence would leave her own life vulnerable to a murderer. One wrong step would be the end—of everything.

She looked at her watch. Seven forty-five. The papers she needed were locked in her desk at *Tempo*. The office was closed, but she still had Maddy's key. She had to get those papers tonight. She finished the coffee with a quick gulp and left a coin on the counter.

She hurried to the corner. A cab slowed down and she got in. They crossed town, then sped up Park Avenue, rushing past the dampness and fog. The cab lurched to a stop. She paid the driver and got out.

The Park Avenue streetlights strained through the fog with bleary eyes. She shivered in the cold and the fog and hurried on. It was odd, she told herself, how things that were once so vital could become so valueless. The past years had added up to minutes of nothingness. But these four months had added up to a whole lifetime. Karen's lifetime. She had seen Karen again through the eyes of Paul and Alan and Mike. And she was able to look at each of them through the eyes of Karen. Now she knew those who loved Karen, those who hated Karen, and the one who had caused Karen's destruction. She wanted the answers. She had found them. She had found more answers than she bargained for.

She held the office key tightly in her hand. She could get the papers she needed now and bring them straight to Mike. He had to have all the proof he could get before tomorrow. There wasn't much time. She had to get to the office and back to Mike tonight before Gerard moved in on him. Gerard said tomorrow. Maybe that was just a stall so he could have her followed. She was well aware that soon someone would be watching her . . . watching every move she made just in case one move was too close to the truth. Someone would watch and wait . . . for the kill. She knew that each shred of evidence she amassed could eventually turn into a violent weapon that might be used to murder her.

CHAPTER 33

The Hewlitt mansion looked empty this time, no streams of light poking out from its heavily curtained windows. The night was almost without sound. There was no movement except her light footsteps hastening up to the entrance. Now she could dimly see the trees that encircled the house and the path that was almost completely enveloped in fog.

As she pressed her finger against the chiming doorbell, Edith thought as long as she lived she would remember the Hewlitt mansion, mysterious and majestic, rising out of fog and shadows into the oblique darkness of night.

The butler showed her into the library. She stood there alone in the massive silence, then moved toward the window and drew an edge of the heavy draperies aside. Her eyes skimmed across the almost invisible pathway to the other side of the street. She leaned closer to the window. She could make out the indistinct form of a man who seemed to be leaning against the fog so that he was almost a part of it. Mike Hewlitt was being watched. She knew the man would be there even before she saw him. Tears moistened her eyes and remained, so that even the night and the streets were a liquid blur, and the faint lights outside became streaks of pale, pale yellow mixed up with the fog and the darkness.

Mike came into the room. He strode across the library to the window where she stood and took her in his arms, and kissed away the tears that were in her eyes.

"Edith," he said. "What's wrong? What's the matter? You look as if you've seen a ghost."

She moved away from the window. "There's a man standing on the opposite side of this street," she said in an odd, flat tone. "He's watching this house."

Mike went to the window and looked out. "I don't see anyone," he said, dropping the curtain.

"But he's there," Edith said. "He's watching you, Mike." That dull, aching fear was strangling her heart again. "They think you killed her, Mike." Her voice rose to a sob.

Mike whitened. "What do you mean?"

"I saw Gerard. They're going to bring you in for questioning." She was still staring numbly at the window.

"That's ridiculous," he said levelly.

"No." Edith drew her eyes back from the draperies. "They found out the suicide note was written long before her death. Alan told them. He said she wrote the note while she was with him just to tell you she was leaving you. Gerard thinks you killed her, you kept the note and placed it next to her body so it would look like suicide." She paused. "You've got to tell them the truth, Mike, don't you see?" She looked at him closely to see if she could detect her own fright mirrored in his eyes.

Mike put his arms around her and led her to a chair. "There's nothing to worry about."

"Yes, there is, Mike," she replied. "I think I know what happened now. And I'm worried. Worried they'll accuse you of murder."

He walked away from her suddenly. His eyes were dark and somber. "Accuse me of murder?" he said angrily. "How can they accuse me when I am innocent?" He turned toward her again and the words he spoke had an undercurrent of resentment. "Is that what you really think, Edith? You think I am guilty?"

"Oh, Mike." She went to him. "No . . . no. You know that I believe in you. I believe in you because I love you. But the police . . . they're not swayed by emotional reasons. They only go on facts."

He frowned with a half-odd angry expression. "I told you the facts. If necessary, I will tell the police the same facts. If they want to know the whole hideous truth—then they shall hear it. She bought that hypo to poison me, not herself."

"But the truth isn't enough," she faltered. "They can say you sent her for the hypo. How would she know it was poison? You could have told her you needed it to develop some pictures. You could have sent her to the drugstore to establish the fact that she made the purchase. They think you planned the whole thing yourself . . . to make it look like suicide."

"Did you forget," he said, "that I have the real suicide note?"

"I didn't forget," Edith said. "But I thought even that might not be enough."

"That suicide note has my signature forged to it," he replied tersely. "Obviously it was intended for me."

She touched his arm anxiously. "But, Mike . . . the police can say you manufactured that as a last resort to save your neck."

He turned away from her angrily. "They can say anything! They can think anything they damn well please!"

She stood there uncertainly, knowing that the necessity to prove his innocence enraged him beyond reason. Yet she knew without a doubt that Gerard had spoken the truth—tonight Mike was being watched. Tomorrow he would be taken in for questioning. The case was reopened. She went to her handbag and took out a piece of paper. "I thought maybe this would help," she said tentatively. "Perhaps this is the proof you need."

He did not look at her. It seemed that he had not even heard her. He had gone to the fireplace and was staring up at the portrait of Karen.

"When you are close to this," he said in a low, even voice, "the face is no longer a face. The body no longer a body. Just thick, massive strokes of black and pink and orange and green and yellow. Bold bright strokes, soft light ones . . . big blobs of color and finely etched lines weaving sinuously in and out and around. It's no one at all," he said. "And yet it lives. It lives here in this house, in this room. It shall live until it destroys me."

"No, Mike!" she cried out. "No. It doesn't live. Karen is dead. She can never destroy you. No one can. We will prove your innocence. We can prove it because I know who is guilty. I know who planned your death. I know who it is, Mike. I know."

His eyes questioned her with dark uncertainty. She couldn't bear to see the pain and the hurt in his face.

"It's Alan," she whispered. "Alan Prescott."

There was a dead silence for a moment. Then he said, "Alan Prescott." Another silence, then: "What makes you say that? Karen and I were the only ones here the night she died."

"Your suicide note—the one you have," she went on urgently, "it's typed on paper from the Chanin agency. From the first, when you showed it to me, there was something about the paper that disturbed me. I went back to my office tonight. I knew that same kind of paper was in my desk. The agency had sent over some memos about the Hewlitt account. It's the same paper, Mike. I'm sure it's the same."

He stared at her. "Why did you have to rake all of this up, Edith? The Hewlitt case was closed. The Hewlitt name protected. And now . . ."

"I'm sorry now, Mike. Terribly sorry. But if I hadn't . . . then I never would have met you," she replied.

Mike said, with a curious catch in his voice, "Better to have loved a suspected murdered than never to have loved at all?"

Tears welled up in her eyes.

"I didn't mean that, Edith. I'm the one who's sorry now. I'll get the paper. It's locked in my room." He turned and quickly strode from the library.

Edith went to the window and moved the draperies aside again. He was there again across the street. A faint shadow . . . waiting . . . and watching. She trembled. Silent voices in the night seemed to be echoing Gerard's words. Mike Hewlitt could be guilty of murder. She dropped the curtain quickly to close out the night . . . its grim shadows . . . silent accusations.

Mike came back into the room with the typed suicide note in his hand. She took it from him and held the two pages next to each other in front of a light. "Look at the watermarks on the paper." She traced the lines with her finger.

He leaned forward. "It's the same paper, all right," he said in a strained voice.

"Memo paper from the Chanin agency," she said. "The page you have is shorter. The top was cut off right there where the letterhead is."

Mike drew back. "If Prescott is guilty . . . why would he use this paper?" he asked himself aloud. "He's too smart for that, unless . . ." Mike stopped, his jaw muscles were drawn into a knot. "Of course," he went on slowly. "He had to use this paper to get someone in the art department to forge my signature. The Chanin agency has used my signature many times for various endorsements." He held the paper up to the light again. "It looks as though it was done with India ink." He traced the curves of ink with his finger. "You can see where the pen marks stop and start again."

Edith leaned over and looked at the paper. "We've got it, Mike.

This is the proof you need. He gave Karen this paper and she typed the words above your signature."

"It was done on my typewriter, all right," he said thoughtfully. "The type matches exactly. Even the small 'a' that always jumps out of line." He looked up from the paper. "But why . . . why would Prescott want to kill me? If Prescott was the man she was going to marry, why was it necessary for them to plot my murder? She could have gone for a divorce whether she had my consent or not." He paused. "The motive—it's staring me right in the face." His lips curled. "Of course. The motive is money. Maybe he didn't even want Karen except to use her to carry out his scheme. But he had to marry her to get his hands on the money she would inherit."

Edith breathed the words softly: "They must have planned it that night in the restaurant. She asked the waiter for some notepaper. Alan told her what to write, then she copied it over later on your typewriter."

Mike said, "Prescott was clever. By telling Gerard it was a 'goodbye' note, not a suicide note—he cleverly manipulated suspicion in my direction. Alan Prescott," he said bitterly. "So Madison Avenue's Pal Joey planned my demise. How disappointed he must have been when his little murder plot boomeranged, and Karen drank the poison by mistake. All that money turned out to be just a mirage. And now," Mike went on, "now he's planning my demise in another way. I had no idea Prescott was so inventive. His latest plot is to get me arrested for murder. Quite an interesting switch, isn't it?"

"But it won't work, Mike." Edith picked up the two papers. "You've got your proof now, all the proof you need to implicate Alan Prescott."

He looked at the papers in her hand for a long moment. Then he replied, "And that won't work either, Edith."

"What do you mean?"

"This isn't proof enough."

Her eyes clouded. "But the paper . . . the paper is the same. It's from the Chanin agency. Anyone can see that, Mike. Of course it's proof." Her voice was steady and cool, not like the sickening thumping of her heart.

"I can't go to the police with this," he said. "It still isn't tangible evidence even if all of it is true."

"Why not?" she pleaded. "Why not, Mike?"

"Because," he answered slowly, "I also could have had memo paper from the Chanin agency."

Her heart sank. She knew he was right. It was a sorry anticlimax to her triumphant deduction. They stood there staring at each other, the papers in her hand between them. There was no way to prove the link between Karen and Alan. No way to prove they had planned the murder of Mike Hewlitt.

Later, his car brought her home. But even in her own apartment she couldn't close out the threatening darkness. She kept seeing the man in the fog near the Hewlitt mansion, and the night with its accusing, watchful eyes.

CHAPTER 34

It was Tuesday evening, December 10, and it was six o'clock, a lonely time to take a chance on a lifetime, Edith thought as she left her office and walked over to Park Avenue. It was still early enough to avoid the streets that would bring her closer to Alan Prescott's apartment.

She always hated six o'clock—when time became a dividing line between those who belonged to someone and those who didn't. The non-belongers stood out sharply then. They were the misplaced persons who clung together in their own clique of solitude because they had no one to go home to, or no one they wanted to go home to. They became the loose end fringe who killed the sad and lonely and frightening hour of six with stiff martinis to bridge the gap between the going and the coming and the nowhere. They were the ones who crowded the bars and jammed the bistros. Six o'clock. The pulsebeat of loneliness.

She walked now so that her steps coordinated with the rhythm of six o'clock that was chiming its hour high on some building towering over mid-Manhattan. One, two, three, four, five, six, she counted slowly, then checked her watch to make sure it coordinated with the time. She moved the tiny hands back three minutes. She cherished every extra minute that belonged to her now.

The lovely, sudden sight of Christmas trees rising up in the center of Park Avenue projected her nostalgia for Christmas in New York. The trees had just been lighted two days ago and now they shimmered in vertical brilliancy, stretching their way through the middle of the Avenue as far as the eye could see. An oasis of beauty in the midst of noise and motors and smoke and cold.

As she walked on she could see the windows of the Grand Central Building lighted to form the outline of a cross hanging high and shining at the end of the islands far above the hurrying masses. Its shape was a majestic cathedral above and beyond the noise and the traffic. It was a wondrous sight, a scene that could only happen in New York.

The scene around her submerged to another one that she had visualized all day. It was a morbid scene—one that had probably transpired at Gerard's office today. Perhaps this scene was still being played out—Gerard's questions, Mike's answers that really weren't answers at all, but just troubled, vague replies that sounded, as truth sometimes does sound, more strange than real. She could see the sad, lost look in Mike's eyes once again as he must have sat there in silent outrage that the innocent must prove his innocence.

Slowly, she turned west on Fifty-fourth Street, threading her way through multitudes of people who were leaving their office buildings. Alan had been very anxious to see her tonight when she phoned him from the office. She knew he would be. He still wasn't sure how much she really knew. But he was going to find out tonight. She was going to confront him with the truth. Accuse him with facts that perhaps would force his confession—or force him to kill her. But she would be safe enough in his apartment. If necessary, she could tell him Mike knew where she was, even though no one knew. If she had told anyone what her plans were—they would surely have tried to stop her.

Yes, it would be most inconvenient for Alan to try to murder her there, she thought sardonically. Too obvious. Too implicating. If he were going to make an attempt on her life, he would have to try it in her apartment and make it look like suicide. Suicide. It must run in the family.

She approached the building where he lived. Her hand trembled as she pressed the button for the elevator. Nothing can happen, she told herself. Nothing can happen. Not to me. But the steps she took from the elevator to his apartment were those of a condemned person walking toward execution.

He opened the door with a drink in his hand and an empty smile on his face. How did I ever find him attractive? she asked herself. Then, almost simultaneously: Fool that I am to have found him at all.

She forced a responding smile as she entered the room and he took her coat. The smile remained set on her face as he went through the usual genialities of his welcome. He motioned toward a chair and she sat down, then he said something about a drink and she shook her head negatively, while all the time he stood talking and sipping his drink with his eyes steadily upon her.

"Are you sure I can't fix you a drink?" he asked her.

She shook her head again and folded her hands in her lap . . . waiting . . . wondering . . . afraid to speak.

He sat down opposite her and leaned forward in his chair. His face suddenly took on a mask of undimensional flatness. "Something's the matter," he said sharply. "What is it?"

The fear raced through her body and reached her throat and constricted it. She could not utter a sound.

"It's about Karen, isn't it?" he said with cunning perception. "For God's sake, Edith . . . don't just sit there. Say something. This isn't Twenty Questions. I can't carry the dialogue all night."

"I'm . . . I'm sorry, Alan." She had found her voice at last. "You're right. It is about Karen."

"Well . . . spill it then. You know we're in this thing together." His voice warmed to the intimacy of the suggestion.

"No, Alan," she managed to say with a minimum of composure. "Not together. You're in this alone."

"What the devil are you getting at?" he asked impatiently.

"I was so absorbed in the question of my own identity," she said, "that I neglected to question yours. I think that you . . . you are the guilty one." Her voice broke in spite of herself.

He laughed then, a long loud, hearty laugh. Then he stopped laughing and a hardness set into his face. "Suppose you tell me what I am guilty of," he said caustically. And it seemed to her that someone else had asked that same question, and she could see Mike's face with its tired lines and she could hear Mike's voice utter those very same words.

"I think," she went on more steadily, "that you and Karen planned to kill Mike Hewlitt. Karen was going to poison him, then go away with you! But something went wrong. Karen drank the glass with the poison in it that was intended for Mike."

"Do you realize what you're saying?" He wasn't laughing now.

"I know what I'm saying, Alan. And I have evidence that proves it."

He put his glass down and reached for a cigarette. He tapped the cigarette sharply on the table. Then he made sure there were no loose shreds of tobacco. Next he took a lighter from his pocket, a thin, flat, silver lighter, and with a quick motion flicked up a flame and held it to the cigarette that he had placed between his lips. He had made a production of lighting that cigarette, a very long production.

"Oh, I see," he said slowly after he had taken the first drag. "And are you going to tell me what this evidence is, or do we have to play Twenty Questions again?"

"Yes. I'm going to tell you, Alan. That's why I wanted to see you tonight. To tell you." She paused and took a breath. "Before Karen died she wrote me a letter. In that letter she said she didn't have to worry about a divorce anymore. She was going to remarry and be in Paris at the end of this month on her honeymoon. Karen wrote that letter to me the day before she died, Alan. Whoever she planned to marry knew that Mike Hewlitt would be out of the way. There could be no divorce because Mike was going to be murdered and the police were going to think it was suicide."

The smile, the ugly, smug smile, was back on his face. "Now, really, Edith . . ."

"Really," she repeated, her heart thumping. "You were the man, Alan. You helped Karen write that suicide note. You had Mike's signature forged on agency paper. You and Karen planned this together so you could get his money." Edith stopped. She was shaken at what she had said, shaken by the fear of reprisal.

A ghost of a smile remained on his lips. He got up and pushed back his chair, making a precise to-do about the angle of a lamp on a table nearby. "This is really so preposterous, so fantastic . . . I just don't know what to say to you. I wouldn't even dignify this ludicrous accusation with a denial." He sat down on the chair again. "The only obvious conclusion to your hysterical outburst," he went on calmly, "is that you have discovered that Hewlitt is guilty. Possibly you're transferring your feelings about Hewlitt over to me. You would like a hunk of all that gold and, after all" —he held up his hands—"as I told you once before, it's out of the question for you to marry a murderer."

She felt her face grow flaming red. "Is that your only defense?" she said, trembling.

"Sorry," he apologized. "You forced me into that one. But what else do you expect me to say, Edith? So Karen wrote you she was going away with a new husband. Maybe she was. But I can assure you I wasn't it. She had a dozen on the string. It was sort of a hobby with Karen—other men. She played. You know that. Hewlitt probably found out she was really leaving him this time and he poisoned her." Then he yawned. "I'm starving," he said. "It's way past dinnertime. How about a good steak at the Pen and Pencil? But I'm going to fix you a drink first. You sure could use a drink, girl." He started toward the kitchen.

"But the suicide note . . ." Edith faltered. She was completely crushed by his reaction. He didn't even have the decency to show concern. He was just . . . bored. Bored and . . . hungry.

Alan turned back. "Oh, that. I was with her when she wrote it. She walked out on him about two weeks before she was found dead. We had dinner together that night and she wrote it at the table. Gerard showed it to me. It's the same note, all right. It was intended to be her goodbye—but not her last goodbye." He nodded with approval. "I never thought Hewlitt was all that clever. I really underestimated the man. He almost got away with it. But Gerard is probably on his tail right now." With that he walked into the kitchen.

She could hear the clink of glasses. Even if he was putting hypo into her drink this minute, it wouldn't rouse her from her state of confusion. She felt like a diver on the brink who had finally taken the excruciating plunge and landed with a dull, flat thud.

Suddenly the phone on the desk rang. She jumped. The penetrating shrill startled her out of her lethargy.

Alan called to her from the kitchen. "Pick it up, will you, and take the message."

She lifted the receiver and held it to her ear. "Hello?" she inquired fragilely into the white mouthpiece.

"Mrs. Prescott?" the pleasant female voice asked. "Mrs. Alan Prescott?"

"What?" Edith mumbled into the phone.

"Mrs. Alan Prescott," the voice went on politely.

"No . . . there's no one . . . I mean . . ." Edith stammered.

The voice in the wire broke in. "Could you take a message, please? This is the Prescott residence, isn't it?"

"Yes . . . yes."

"Well, this is Pan American Airlines. Could you please give a message to Mrs. Prescott?" The voice went on hastily: "The tickets she reserved under the names of Karen and Alan Prescott have to be picked up this Friday. She made two reservations May 8—for Pan American's World Flight No. 273 leaving December 24. She left a deposit, but we have to have the full payment by next Friday. Would you give her that message, please?"

"Yes." Edith put the phone back together again and stared blankly at the white instrument that had just conveyed the enigmatic message.

"Who was that?" Alan called out from the kitchen.

"Nothing . . . nothing," she called back. The numbness was beginning to disseminate with a prickly feeling like a sleeping foot that had just awakened. "It . . . it was just a wrong number."

Alan walked into the living room with two drinks in his hand. But her eyes were riveted on the white telephone. Her mind was spinning like a roulette wheel with its shiny silver ball bouncing in and out of the narrow slots. The minute ball hopped around slowly, slowly . . . then rolled into a permanent niche. It was settled. Firmly settled. Irrevocably settled. Pan American Airlines had provided the missing link. It was an act of God. An act of chance. A gamble won. Pan American Airlines, thank their corporate hearts, had evidence that proved Prescott plotted Mike's murder with Karen. They had it all written down on a slip of paper that Alan knew he was going to Paris as Karen's next husband. He knew it before the fact. Because he knew Mike Hewlitt was going to be among the deceased. He knew it because he planned it. Now she just needed one more chance to be safe. The chance to send out this latest communiqué to the police. She prayed the odds would be with her again.

Alan had handed her a drink. She sipped it cautiously, but it only tasted like the usual 86-proof scotch. Hypo apparently wasn't in his line this time.

"C'mon," he said, "let's drink up and hit the road." He downed his drink rapidly and she rose to get her coat.

Suddenly the ringing of the phone again. She made a motion toward the desk as if to answer it again.

"I'll get it," he said quickly. He set his glass down and reached for the receiver at the same time.

"Hello?" he said into the phone. She stood there waiting.

"Yes," he said, and paused. "Prescott speaking."

A few seconds of silence. She could hear the faint jumbled sounds of words coming from the cup part he had pressed to his ear.

"Uh-huh. Yes." Another pause. She couldn't make out whether the voice on the wire was masculine or feminine.

"Certainly," he said. "Thank you very much." He hung up the phone and turned to her.

"All set?" He smiled, grabbing his coat. "Then let's go."

When they reached the street he signaled a cab and a few minutes later they drew up along the curb next to the Pen and Pencil. She was safe now, perfectly safe. There were two shiny round dimes in her pocketbook. Sometime during the meal she would excuse herself and go to the powder room. Two lovely silver dimes . . . her sesame to security. She could reach Mike now and Gerard. Two phone calls. Even one would be enough. Did anyone ever dream that a ten-cent piece could be the difference between life and death?

It wasn't. She went to the powder room but there were no telephones in sight. She even had a chance to ask the headwaiter. Then a few minutes later a beaming maître d' plugged in the phone right at the table where they were sitting. In feverish, fumbling haste, under the watchful eyes of her escort, she dialed Maddy's number. She listened to the "no answer" signal with mixed feelings of despair, fear, and anguish. She glanced at Alan furtively. He made no comment. But as she slowly hung up the phone there was a sardonic smile on his face.

CHAPTER 35

He shoved his gray felt hat way back on his forehead. A cigarette languorously hung from his lips. "Aren't you even going to ask me up for a nightcap?" He was leaning against the outside wall of the building, leisurely and assured.

Her fingers curled around the edges of her black coat and she drew it closer. "I'm terribly sorry," she said quickly, "but it's rather late." She glanced toward the entrance of her apartment house but no one was in sight. Even traffic had dissipated and the sounds of cars could just be heard from what seemed like an infinite distance.

"It's only ten," Alan said, looking at his watch. "Since when do you punch a time clock?"

"Since now. I have to be at the office early tomorrow." She edged closer to the entrance of the building.

"I see." He stamped out his cigarette with his foot. "I recall way back in the olden days when time wasn't of the essence to you," he drawled sarcastically.

He had followed her to the entrance and the light from within focused on the two of them. He was looking at her curiously, tentatively. She took two steps backward, further into the inner sanctum of the entrance hall.

Then he laughed. Involuntarily she shuddered. His laughter for some curious reason had the ring of an insidious knowing. What secret did he possess now that was so exclusive? He stepped up close to her, almost against her.

"Okay," he murmured in an offhand way. "So go home if that's what you want. If you're sure that's what you want," he amended suggestively, holding her with his eyes.

She pulled her eyes away from his and started walking fast further inside the building. He trailed after her for a few steps, then stood there and watched her as she pressed the elevator button. She managed a smile and a faint "Thank you for the dinner," then looked up to watch the indicator above the elevator signal its descent. Five . . . four . . . three . . . two . . . one. Thank God. It landed. The doors automatically rolled aside and a lavishly dressed fat woman in a mink coat walked out carrying three bundles. Thank God, too, for the fat woman in the mink coat and the three bundles. Edith stepped inside the elevator while the woman was nearing the entrance to the street. She jabbed at the button for the sixth floor. The elevator doors paused.

"Don't call me, sweetie," Alan's voice crept into the elevator cage with innuendo. "I'll call you."

The doors slowly rolled toward each other and finally met with a soft clack and the elevator was on the rise.

She could feel the beads of perspiration on her forehead although her face was still cold from the night. She was shaking. Even now the shaking wouldn't stop, even though she was safe. Almost home and safe.

The elevator jolted to a stop and the doors rolled open again and she got out and dug into her bag for the door key. Six more steps to home. She started to take them on the run.

The key turned in the lock. The door swung open and she stepped into the darkness. She fumbled for the light switch in the foyer and the click illuminated the tiny entrance. She wiped her forehead with her hand, then stood very still. She had to stand still. Maybe that would stop the trembling, because she felt she would suddenly die of a heart attack and that would be the ultimate irony of all.

In a sudden movement she ran back to the front door and bolted the safety lock. She pulled the door to make sure it was locked, locked tight. She leaned against the door for a moment and tried to catch her breath. Calm, cool, and collected. She kept running the words together over and over again so her pulsebeat would listen and not keep racing along like an idiot. It was beginning to get the message. She sighed with relief. Now I have to phone Mike, she thought. Well, do it, do it, do it.

She opened the door from the foyer that led right into the kitchen and picked up the telephone that was on the table. The dial was clearly visible in the stream of light from the foyer.

Her hand was just about to touch it, her finger outstretched pointing toward the dial, when it rang. Suddenly, alarmingly, it rang. Her heart leapt and started up in terror. She took the receiver off with trembling hands. She felt as if the telephone had caught her in a criminal act.

"Hello?" Her own voice sounded queer to her.

"Edith . . . this is Mike." His voice was low, mumbled, hoarse. "I've been trying to reach you all evening. Where've you been? Edith? Edith?" he whispered frantically.

"Thank God," she sobbed to the phone and to the voice.

"What's wrong?"

"Listen, Mike," she said into the phone, "listen. It was Alan. I found out it was Alan," she rushed on almost incoherently. "They made a reservation. Pan American. They have proof he was going to marry her. They bought two tickets as man and wife in May. Do you understand, Mike? We have the proof now. The proof." Her voice rose in panic.

"Okay," she heard him say softly. Then . . . a mumble of words.

"I can't hear you, Mike. There's something wrong with this connection."

"I said," he repeated, "does anyone else know?" The voice sounded far away.

"No one knows. No one."

There was a pause. Then the voice on the wire murmured urgently: "Just stay there, Edith. I'll be right over. Don't let anyone— not anyone—into the apartment. Keep your door locked. Don't answer the phone. Pretend you're out. If Prescott has any idea you know this, he'll try to kill you. Can you hear me?" he whispered.

"Yes," she said. "Yes. I understand. Hurry. Please hurry. I'm frightened." She hung up the phone and walked slowly out of the kitchen across the foyer and into the living room. It was while her hand was on the lamp, on the tiny switch at the base of the lamp, that she stopped. She stopped and her hand froze on the spot and she stared. In the shadows of the living room, back against the draperies, she made out a hulking form. She stopped, her body leaning over, her hand poised just on the lamp switch, and she froze. Then she screamed. She screamed and screamed and screamed.

The horrible thing took two steps forward in the darkness toward her. She stood quite still, her hands clutching and unclutching at the coat she still wore. She dared not breathe, she dared not utter a sound. It was moving to the table now near the draperies, and its hands were pawing the lamp on the table. How many seconds did she have to live? How many seconds did she have to come face to face with her murderer? No panorama of her life flashed in montage before her eyes as the last gesture afforded those who are about to die. All that was afforded her in these brief seconds was the inane repetition of three words that were whispering inside of her—this is it, this is it, this is it, this is it.

Suddenly, a soft light bounced into the corner of the darkness near the windows. The form moved closer to her. It had taken shape at last. She found herself staring into the eyes of Lieutenant Gerard of the New York Homicide Division.

A sob strangled in her throat. The silence remained intact. Then finally he spoke.

"I'm terribly sorry, Miss Weston," his low voice rumbled on in apology. "I sure didn't mean to scare you to death."

She looked at him blankly and remained rooted on the spot.

"I was afraid to call out," he kept on with the apology. "I thought that would make it even worse in the dark." He shifted his feet awkwardly, his hat held sheepishly in his hand. Gerard looked odd and uncomfortable out of his bailiwick. The kindly, impassive face for once was registering a helpless concern. For the first time he didn't seem to know what to do or say. He was almost pathetic in his misery.

Edith slowly removed her coat and threw it on the chair. She found her voice at last. It was a weak, foggy voice but at least a voice. Better than nothing.

"I don't know what you're doing here. I don't know how you managed to get into my apartment, and I certainly can't imagine why you were hiding near the curtains in the darkness . . . but . . ." Then her face relaxed. "Won't you have a drink and sit down?"

Gerard eased himself into a chair. "No drink, thanks. I'm on duty. But maybe you better have that drink. You look as if you need one."

"No, thank you." She sat down opposite him.

Gerard ran his fingers through his light sparse hair and concern revisited his face. "You see, Miss Weston . . . I wasn't really expecting you. I heard the key turn in the lock. I knew someone had entered the apartment. But I didn't know it was you until I heard you answer the phone. Then I figured if I called out at that moment the person you were talking to would know I was here. So I did the only thing I could do. I kept still."

Edith glanced at him quizzically. "Whom were you expecting, Lieutenant?"

He frowned. "I'm not quite sure."

"I'm afraid I'm not following you," she said, bewildered.

"But we were following you, Miss Weston. We know you were out with Prescott tonight. Regan—you met him in my office, remember?—well, Regan was keeping an eye on you. I was waiting here just in case you invited Prescott in. I suppose you realize now that you do need police protection."

"Invite him in? I couldn't get away fast enough." She paused. "I thought he might . . . there was a chance he might have tried to kill me." She fingered her black dress nervously. "That's what you were afraid of, wasn't it?"

"Possibly."

"Only possibly?" she asked, her eyebrows lifting. "Do you know what I found out tonight? I answered the phone in his apartment earlier this evening. It was Pan American. He had made a reservation in May for a honeymoon trip with Karen. That phone call proves he knew Mike Hewlitt was going to be out of the way. It proves that he and Karen planned to kill Mike and make it look like suicide."

"Um," Gerard grunted. "We knew about the Pan American reservation."

"You *knew?*" The edge of a hysterical laugh broke through her lips. "All this time . . . you *knew?*"

"No, just recently. We have to play detective too, Miss Weston," Gerard said in almost sheepish apology. "We checked December plane reservations to Paris after you gave us your sister's letter."

"Then what are you waiting for?" she cried out. "You have all the proof you need. Just arrest Alan Prescott!"

"It's proof that Prescott intended to go to Paris with Karen . . . yes. But it doesn't prove conspiracy to murder Mike Hewlitt, nor does it prove how Karen Hewlitt died."

"Then I accomplished nothing," she said tonelessly. Everything was for nothing. She was defeated. Completely defeated.

"You managed to reopen the Hewlitt case," Gerard said encouragingly. "And that took quite a bit of doing." He cleared his throat. "Um, yes. Quite a bit." He took a cigar out of his pocket and stared at it thoughtfully. "That phone call just now . . . was that Mike Hewlitt?"

"Why, yes," she said uneasily. "He just wanted to make sure I was all right."

Gerard held a light to the cigar. Then he suddenly blew the match out. "I'd better not smoke in here. I almost forgot."

"Go ahead," she said automatically.

"Thank you. But the cigar smoke would be a dead giveaway. In case you have a visitor," he added, putting the cigar back in his pocket with reluctance.

Edith's heart started to pound away again. "What . . . what are you getting at?"

"Well, it's like this," Gerard replied slowly. "You wanted to set yourself up as a pigeon, Miss Weston, right from the start. And you did. You did by asking too many questions, finding too many answers. And"—he paused—"and getting involved with two people. Alan Prescott and Mike Hewlitt. That's two too many. Everything you said about Prescott may be true."

She breathed with relief.

"And then again, it may not be. The same goes for Hewlitt. Maybe his wife's death was accidental poisoning. Maybe she did try to murder him with Prescott as an accomplice to the planned crime. Maybe yes, and maybe no. There's only one way of proving either story. That's why I'm here tonight. You went too far. We believe an attempt on your life will be made tonight by the guilty party. Both Prescott and Hewlitt are in this neighborhood now. We think the guilty one will come here tonight and try to kill you."

There was a long pause. Edith's heart flipped over. "But Mike . . ." she said hollowly. "Mike is going to be here. He just told me on the phone. I was even going to call him."

"But he got to you first, eh?" Gerard moved uncomfortably in the too small chair.

"Why should Mike—" She broke off abruptly. "I can understand about Alan. He thinks I'm the only one who has all the pieces put together. I even told him why he was guilty. He has to get to me before I talk. Even though he isn't aware that Pan American was on the phone, I still know too much for comfort. But Mike—" She let it hang in the air.

Gerard grabbed it down with decision. "But Mike Hewlitt," he said, "could have poisoned Karen. He was there. And there was no way he could verify his story today. He might have manufactured the whole thing—even the typed letter with his name on it. He could have cleverly arranged that as a last resort—a sort of life insurance policy."

"But we know Alan was going to marry Karen. The plane tickets and the letter prove that. It also gives us his motive," Edith persisted. "Mike Hewlitt doesn't even have a motive."

"On the contrary." Gerard rubbed his chin. "Mike Hewlitt had a very strong motive for murder. He could have discovered that Prescott and his wife planned to kill him and go away together. So he poisons his wife in self-defense."

"The fingerprints . . ." Edith protested.

"You don't have to handle a glass to drop poison into it."

"But the bottle . . ."

Gerard waved the words aside. "Hewlitt could have engineered a plot to avoid all suspicion. Mrs. Hewlitt's prints would naturally be on the bottle if she made the purchase for him. We have to suspect Hewlitt. Can't you understand that, Miss Weston?"

"I'm trying to," she answered with difficulty.

"If he can hate enough to kill his wife, then he can hate enough to kill you. You know too much, Miss Weston. You knew Karen wasn't planning suicide . . . she was planning to go away with another man. And you made the fatal mistake of telling Hewlitt that was in her letter to you. He knows if it weren't for you—this whole Hewlitt mess would still be in the inactive files. It seems to me he would go to any extreme to protect the Hewlitt name . . . or wreak vengeance on anyone who attempted to derogate it."

CHAPTER 36

The words clung to the room. She had a premonition that Gerard was right. The person who rang that doorbell was going to try to kill her. Was it going to be Mike? The thought was insufferable. She couldn't bear trying to tear apart the tangled fringes of suspicion and speculation any longer. She glanced at her watch. She wished the doorbell would ring and the murderer announce himself and get it over with. She couldn't live like this any longer. This living was only a long process of dying. She looked around at the slickly decorated room. It would be difficult for the readers of *Tempo* to envision this background as a setting for murder. Too bad it was so late. She could have phoned the staff photographer. Still, it was such a lovely apartment. Rather incongruous for the scene of the crime.

Gerard stood up. It was as if, in some infinitesimal way, he sensed the time for waiting was almost over.

"I'll be waiting in the kitchen," he said softly, and moved his bulky body along with the words. He gently patted the bulge in his right pocket and turned toward her. "You won't have to worry, Miss Weston. Like I told you—you set yourself up as a pigeon. But I have no intention of letting you become a dead pigeon." He turned and walked across the foyer and stepped out of sight into the dark cubicle of a kitchen. He hadn't disappeared a moment too soon.

She heard the faint sound of the elevator, slow, measured footsteps, then louder ones, quicker ones. They stopped just outside the door. She looked at her trembling hands. They were chalk white. As white as death itself.

The doorbell rang shrilly. She could not move from her seat. She was petrified. Answer it, answer it, answer it, she told herself silently. Someone was banging on the door. She thought she heard him calling her name. The doorbell rang again, then the pounding on the door. Answer it, answer it, the silent voice was urging her, then it will all be over. Over at last. The banging on the door became louder and louder. As in a dream she moved . . . so slowly, so easily toward the door and the ringing and the pounding.

"Edith, Edith." Someone was calling her name through the closed door. The voice came through in an urgent whisper. "It's Mike. Open the door."

Slowly, she unlocked the lock. She put her hand on the doorknob and turned it. The door swung open.

Alan Prescott shoved past her inside the foyer. He locked the door after him. The color had drained from her face. She stood there looking at him without saying a word.

He pushed her ahead of him into the living room. Hatred narrowed his eyes, tightened the muscles of his jaws, even changed his voice. His words jerked out, breathless. "Yes, I was Mike on the phone. I wanted to make sure you had told no one. Had seen no one. Until I got here."

He flung his coat on the chair. "I knew you didn't buy my story. Not for a minute. I knew it even before you tried to make a phone call in that restaurant." He hissed out the phrases rapidly. "Get out of town, before it's too late, my love . . . I warned you."

"You sent the record . . . you were in that car. It was you all the time, it was you!"

Then he stepped closer to her. She shut her eyes tight and prayed to God and prayed to Lieutenant Gerard and prayed to the gun in Gerard's pocket.

"The second phone call in my apartment was . . . Pan American calling back." He was speaking slowly now, clearly, as if to let his words sink in and destroy her before he destroyed her himself. "They rang back because they forgot about the deposit slip." He laughed a short, ugly, hideous laugh. "Edith Weston," he went on bitterly as she stood there not daring to breathe, not daring to move. "Edith Weston—the supersleuth. You were right. I planned Hewlitt's murder with Karen. I was going to marry her. To get hold of that mint . . . why not? I composed the suicide note and Karen rewrote it on his typewriter. And the forged signature . . . I told someone in the art department I needed it for an endorsement." He paused, then said admiringly, "It was a perfect setup for murder. Except for Karen's stupid, fatal error. She drank out of the wrong glass." The horrible laugh again. "I should have known better than to trust a woman. I even phoned her that night just to check. She told me everything was ready. That meant she had put the poison in his glass." Alan shook his head. "And all Hewlitt had to do was drink it." He cursed contemptuously. "But when the police said Karen's death was suicide instead of accidental poisoning —I got worried. I figured Hewlitt maybe suspected that I was implicated, that I was going to marry her, that I put her up to the murder, that he was going to get even with me. But he reinstated the account, so I knew I was safe. He was too busy protecting the Hewlitt name to tell anyone she was going to poison him. Her suicide story that he dreamed up suited the police and me just fine. Too bad it didn't suit you, Edith. I played that long shot to win and I lost. But now I stand a chance of losing everything. Everything I struggled for, fought for, sweated for . . . my career, job, life . . . everything out the window." He stopped, then added, *"Or you out the window*. It's your life against mine, Edith. What choice would you take?"

"No . . . no," she mumbled frantically. "No."

"Another suicide for Lieutenant Gerard. But this case is going to stay closed." He pushed her violently back against the wall. The room was all mixed together, huge blobs of color, slashed shreds of ribbons. He picked up the iron tongs from the fireplace and started to back her toward the windows. She heard a window go up. Streaks of pain flashed through her body, a hard slap across her face. Her body was half over the ledge of the window. She felt sudden gusts of cold air. She heard herself scream but the scream was too faint, too far away. Then came mumbled voices. She was dragging her way back to the sofa now and the tears were starting to spill, splashing down her cheeks, down, right into little dots of wetness on the carpet. The sobs came faster now and her shoulders started to heave and the tears were washing away some of the pain and the hurt that had mingled with the numbness. Some other men had entered the apartment. Noise and confusion. Voices. More noise. It was getting farther away now . . . fainter. Someone held a glass of water to her lips and a tiny white pill.

She didn't know how long she sat there, but finally everything was quiet and she could see that Detective Regan was sitting opposite her. Then her tears stopped and she sat there staring numb and blank, and that was far worse than the tears.

Then Regan said to her quietly, "It's all right now, Miss Weston.

We've got him this time. Prescott is through. He's been arrested for attempted murder. Too bad you had to be the target for tonight."

She shook her head silently and twisted her hands in her lap.

"This clears Hewlitt," Regan was saying. "That phone conversation Prescott told you he had the night Mrs. Hewlitt died, verifies the fact that Mrs. Hewlitt herself placed the poison in the glass." He shook his head. "Karen Hewlitt died of accidental poisoning. No one legally is responsible for her death. But off the record you might say that Prescott was in a way guilty of that too."

The doorbell rang and Edith jumped up with fear in her eyes again. Regan stood up and eased her back on the sofa. "It's okay, Miss Weston. That must be Hewlitt now," he said. "Lieutenant Gerard said he was on his way over here."

A man stood in front of her and she looked up at him. The trembling stopped when she heard Mike's low, even voice speaking to her.

"Edith," he said quietly. "It's all right now. Everything is going to be all right." He sat down next to her and took her hand and held it.

Then after a long, long time she began to feel safe again. The tears of tonight were finished with, the ghosts were buried, the questions were answered. The dreams and nightmares had become realities, no longer suspended in space to frighten her. Now she could walk and breathe and listen to the sounds of the cars and the sounds of the night, and the sounds of people's voices and laughter in the streets of the city. They would never be still because in New York it is never really silent and quiet. Even later when the streets are empty, all you have to do is listen, and you will hear the sounds jumbled together into a sort of symphony, a kind of music in the air. She used to think of it as a cacophony. But not now. Not anymore. Not after tonight. She would forget tonight and those other nights, when sounds jarred the senses and came crashing around the ears like a million wrong notes all mixed together. That was New York before. But now it was going to be a wonderful, melodic symphony. These were wonderful sounds because they were sounds of life. She would always hear them from now on.

The story of Karen had finally come to a close. Her life and death could be buried now for all time. There would be no postmortems. There were no mourners. Edith looked toward the window and a light snowfall was gently dotting the pane. Karen was buried in the night, and buried with her was the part of Edith that wanted to be Karen, a part that for a while lived even as Karen had lived. Now that had died too.

There was a sadness, a tragedy in the truth that could never be obliterated. Karen was dead and that was the end. But it was an end that triggered a beginning. And Edith knew that everything would be different now. Nothing would ever be quite the same. Yesterday was gone. Tonight was over. She could look for tomorrow. It seemed strange to begin at the end. But it was her beginning at last.

While *Living Image* is Gladys S. Gallant's first novel, she authored many teleplays and original dramas for the major networks, and was a member of the CBS staff program writing department for television and radio for ten years. Ms. Gallant also wrote for the Foote, Cone, and Belding advertising agency and her articles have appeared in *Good Housekeeping* and *Glamour* magazines. In addition, Ms. Gallant was an accomplished artist and had a one-man show at the Gallerie Internationale in Manhattan. She also received the Joey Award for distinguished service for the Children's Asthma Research Institute, parade of stars. Ms. Gallant lived with her husband and daughter in New York. She died shortly after the completion of this novel.